Gentry *Red* Redmond gave up on finding a mate. It turns out the one he needed just didn't come in the package he was used to hunting.

Sebastian Del Marco, a traveling nurse, wants to be loved, but he's afraid to trust. Instead of relationships, he's been willing to accept just having fun.

Once Red realizes Sebastian is just the mate he needs, can he convince Sebastian to take a chance on love?

Flirty and Red
Copyright © 2022 Deja Black
ISBN: 978-1-4874-3254-6
Cover art by Martine Jardin

Published by eXtasy Books Inc.

Look for us online at:
www.eXtasybooks.com

Flirty and Red
Children of the Sun 1

By

Deja Black

DEDICATION

For Ericka.
Thank you for believing in me, never saying no to reading another
one, and gently kicking my ass when I second guess myself just
one more time.

Deja

CHAPTER ONE

R ed glanced around at the people in the gun store's training room: grandmothers, nearly teenagers, burly grand-
pas, teachers, and the like. No two people looked the same,
and he didn't know their names. Rows of long rectangular tables filled the room with one or two participants at each. It
reminded him of his old science classes, but instead of some
poor amphibian prepared for dissection, the instructor laid an
example of a dismantled gun on the table with a stack of
forms next to it. Red glanced at the gun and back to the motley
class of people surrounding him.

Yeah, there were a few in here he knew didn't need to get
a concealed weapons license, much less own a gun, but he
wasn't going to worry about them. Instead, he needed to get
this done, get to the gym, check on the shipment, and call his
father. His father and his fear of the current Ilios was the reason he was here, after all. Why would the Ilios, their clan
leader, think capturing Red like a pawn on a chessboard
would be the right thing to do?

They were griffins, children of the sun. It was their duty to
protect knowledge and to guide humankind. But instead of
being guided by the light, their Ilios had driven Red's family
into darkness.

*Get your license. Protect yourself. Our people are coming, and
you need to be ready. This Ilios is different. He doesn't abide by our
laws. You're not safe.*

A gun, though, had not been his choice. Red knew how to
fight, had trained just like his younger brother Jacobi and

their father before them. But there were those unlike him who'd discarded the rules, choosing the weaker alternative instead.

Where was the Atkina, the ray of the Ilios, in all of this? Shouldn't she help Laith Baher see all of this was wrong? The Ilios was supposed to choose someone strong enough to challenge them, someone who would act as a just extension of the Ilios's power. A person who directed the Stemma, the Ilios's corona. Under the right leader, the Atkina and the soldiers, known as the Stemma, shined a light on the world, giving aid to those who needed it and protecting the weak. Under Laith, they were destructive and fearsome, forcing their people to run and hide.

It didn't matter what course the Ilios had chosen. Red would do what would make his father happy and take the path that would keep his family safe.

Looking over the room, he picked a spot near enough to the front to hear but close enough to the edge he could leave if he needed. Setting his things down, he took a seat.

Settling back, he stretched out his long legs, his steel toe boots pointing upward. At least he was at the front. He was a big guy, and having to squeeze in the back like a few of the other participants would have killed him.

"Hi, I'm Sebastian," his table partner said with his hand sticking out.

Red didn't care what the guy's name was. He wanted to get this training finished. A getting-to-know-you session wasn't on that list.

But his mama hadn't raised him to be disrespectful.

He shook the man's hand. "Red."

"Oh, but the instructor said your name was Gentry Redmond when he went through the list at the check-in. I guess you prefer Red."

Whiskey brown eyes that Red wasn't noticing at all gazed

at him expectantly, and without fail, Red followed through.

"I do."

There, two words. That ought to end it.

"Well, I bet until people learn your last name, they probably think the reason is because of that gorgeous red hair of yours." Sebastian laughed

The sound slid down Red's spine and raced over his nerve endings. The effect touched his beast, and it stirred.

What the hell?

"Huh," was Red's stellar response.

Was the flirty guy wearing lip gloss? His lips were wet and plump.

Kissable, if a body liked kissing a man.

"Well, my name is Sebastian Del Marco. I'm a traveling nurse. What about you?"

"Architect," Red answered.

When exactly was this training supposed to start?

"Okay, you build. I heal. It could almost rhyme if you stretched it out a bit." The man almost danced, gesturing along with his observation.

"So, where you from?" Sebastian asked.

What the hell kind of name is that anyway? Who willingly names their son Sebastian? Should have called him Flirty.

The guy had been talking non-stop so far, chatting Red up. The room wasn't a club, and Red wasn't interested in men, human or not, no matter what his griffin thought. He was barely interested in women.

Hell, Red didn't have the time, with his business increasing. People were interested in building houses. He was interested in getting paid to create them. Being an architect provided a roof over his head and gave him his new truck. His main focus was to be there for his family, help out on the farm, and give his dad solid peace of mind.

Having sex with anyone is the furthest thing from my mind right now. Hang out with the guys? Yes. Do one? No.

He was surprised to learn Flirty was a nurse. The guy would make a hell of a reporter. Maybe one of those entertainment news people the way the questions kept peppering him, seasoning him up with his who, what, when, and where's.

He had to admit that Flirty was a nice-looking guy if someone were checking him out—dark-haired, dark brown eyes, and fit. Seemed to love color and things that sparkled.

He had told someone else about the shirt he wore and how he'd had it bedazzled. Truth was, it wasn't a terrible look on the guy, but it didn't make sense to Red why the outline of the wings needed to sparkle like that. The design was in a dragon's form, the wings poised for flight. It was nicely done and drew attention to the man's trim waist and the muscles that covered his frame, smooth and sleek like a new pony. Red noticed how the sparkles near Flirty's pecs spread out a bit. His tongue might have stuck to the roof of his mouth for a heartbeat at the hint of nipple there.

He cleared his throat and answered Flirty's last question. "I'm from Louisville."

Red had grown up here, lived here every one of his twenty-six years. He didn't see himself moving anywhere. He loved the big city, slow-motion vibe Louisville had. At almost three hundred thousand people, it was Kentucky's largest city, nearly busting at the seams, but it didn't feel like that at all. Anywhere a person wanted to go only took twenty minutes. Louisville was a city of endless circles that all seemed to connect. Nowhere else was like that for him.

Nowhere else was safe for his beast, either. The moment Red found a mate, their people would arrive that much faster. And from the way his father was talking, they weren't going to play nice. If things got dicey, he knew Louisville like the back of his hand. As their home turf, it gave him and his family the upper hand if a battle had to be fought.

Doing what I can to make sure they don't take me by surprise.

Red picked up his water bottle and sipped, hoping the inability to talk would get Flirty to leave him alone. Inside, his griffin paced, wings pushing against the surface. It had been a while since he'd flown. Lately, there just hadn't been any time.

"Oh, you've been here all your life?" Sebastian continued. "Well, that's nice. I live here for now, but I'm actually from Puerto Rico. My family has a farm there, and I went back to visit some time ago. But, you know, couldn't stay long—too much to do. "

Red smiled and grunted in response, but he didn't say anything. Seemed his mouth filled with water was not a deterrent after all.

His beast was getting restless, and its edginess was driving him crazy. Sebastian was making him a little crazy, too.

Finally, the instructor announced the start of class, and Red couldn't have been more grateful. If he had to be here eight hours, he didn't see how he was gonna make it seated next to Flirty. But if they could get this thing going, he would be that much closer to finished. Finished sounded real good to him.

Red flipped his phone over, glancing at the time. 9:13. He sighed when the instructor went through the list of precautions. If Red had to guess, the older guy was former law enforcement, which meant every *t* would be crossed and *i* dotted.

Red shook his head and looked away when he noticed Flirty nearly vibrating with energy. He didn't have anything against gay people. He just wasn't one of them and didn't see the need to be with a guy, dipping his wick where it wasn't natural when there were plenty of women around. But that didn't stop Flirty from turning to talk to him, all bouncy and energy blazing.

"So, what type of gun did you bring?" Flirty asked, gazing at the box Red had settled next to his water bottle.

"Nine-millimeter." Hell, it was one of several he owned and a recent addition as a gift from his father. The stainless steel Sig Sauer P 226 was a gorgeous piece of work. She was reliable, and her accuracy was without comparison. Right now, she was put away, safe, waiting for her moment to shine.

Red knew how to shoot all of his guns, including the ones stashed on his parent's land. He'd been shooting since he was able to pull his own trigger. New laws, and here he was. Waste of time, but he wasn't about to tell his dad that.

Pick your battles.

"Oh, I just have a gun I borrowed from a friend of mine."

Flirty stared as if waiting for a response, but Red wasn't any more interested in chatting than he had been five seconds ago. Sadly, it was too late to change seats.

Red nodded. Great, not only did the guy talk forever, but he also had a gun he didn't know how to use. There were all kinds of ways that could go wrong. He'd have to be sure to give the man some room on the shooting range, as he wasn't itching for any of those bullets to wear his name.

"It's a Beretta."

Red nodded, then picked up his phone, pretending to find something, anything on it that would let the guy know he wasn't interested in talking. Worked on airplanes.

"I know what you're thinking."

Did he now?

"You're thinking it's the first time I've ever shot a gun, but I'm terrific. I have skills." Flirty laughed.

Red had to admit he liked the sound. It was warm, genuine, and slid along his spine, teasing each one of his bones with a tiny charge.

Before he realized what was happening, the words fell out, "Really? How?" Damn, he hadn't meant to sound doubtful, hadn't meant to say anything at all.

Oh, look at that, the big ginger-haired man finally engaged. Well, Sebastian certainly liked the spark in those hazel eyes. He'd noticed the giant when he'd first walked in, a gladiator sizing up the room, surveying all in his path. The guy was easily 6'4 to Sebastian's 5'8, so he would be a lovely tree to climb. His shirt wrapped biceps as big as honeydew melons, and his dark-colored jeans showcased a plump ass that Sebastian wanted to bite.

Red had gazed at the places around him until he saw the seat he wanted next to Sebastian. And like a warrior king of old, he sat down, commanding the space. The air around them was spicy with Red's scent, and Sebastian inhaled, enjoying the aroma. Woodsy. Manly. He loved it.

Of course Sebastian spoke to him. He talked to everyone. It was what he did, and one of the reasons patients typically requested him. The ability to carry a conversation with very little help and his openness slotted him high on the request list of traveling nurses. His words flowed like a river, heedless of the obstructions along the way. He paid little notice to the scars and hurts, making his own trail of happiness for dancing along as he helped his patients get better.

People who were sick needed companionship, someone who would help them forget their suffering, so they asked for Sebastian.

"Yes, I was in the army for six years." He laughed again when the ginger's eyes widened in surprise, his stomach clenching with how hard those brilliant stunners hit him. He could only imagine where else he'd love to see that look. He would lay down money the man absolutely glowed before he orgasmed. All that bronze skin hidden underneath the blue *Under Armor* pullover would be slick and inviting. He could see the hints of color at his neck, and Sebastian missed nothing.

He also saw the tanning card on the keychain along with

7

the gym membership. Here was a man who cared about appearance, and Sebastian could get behind that.

"Military?"

Sebastian could almost hear the unasked question — *You?*

Oh, baby. This was fun,

Sebastian had no problem answering questions, both the spoken and implied.

"Yes, me." He leaned in, and more of that scent teased him, making him want things he hadn't in a long time, his self-imposed sexual moratorium bearing down on him.

Eight hours next to this guy, he could do.

Seated on Sebastian's other side was a college kid named Corey, who achingly wanted to prove he was an emancipated adult, and Sebastian was all in for him. He'd listened and responded accordingly to the changes Corey had made in his life and his new job. Nodded and laughed, jumping in to celebrate with him. He'd met a few other people in the class, checking in with a girl he went to school with a few years back. He'd ignored the guy who looked like a character from Deliverance. The things that came out of his mouth made Sebastian a little nervous about him carrying any weapon.

But, Gentry *call me Red* Redmond? He was worth paying attention to. Red had been quick to correct the teacher when the guy had tried to use his full name. Sebastian thought Gentry was a lovely name and could picture him, guns at his side, facing off against a villain in a cowboy western. He was all cowboy, with the ballcap he wore propped up, his stride rolling as he walked into the room, and again, the way those jeans wrapped that luscious bottom.

Yep, all cowboy. Sebastian shuddered. His self-imposed sex moratorium was definitely over.

Red's laugh snapped Sebastian out of his daydreams.

Red frowned. "I didn't say — "

"Oh, you didn't have to." Sebastian smiled and enjoyed the way Red's cheeks flushed. "Was in the Army for six years."

"Reserve?" Red asked.

"Yes. Paid for my schooling."

"Yeah, nurse in the Reserves, right? Or at least in medical?"

So, Red had been listening. Sebastian hadn't been sure at first. The man had kept checking his phone but not engaging or actively listening except for when they'd spoken briefly earlier. When Sebastian had Red's full attention, he liked it. It felt like a caress over his skin, a touch in places that ached. He was a greedy bitch and wanted more.

"Yes, my father was military, and my grandfather before him. Naturally, as the only boy, I needed to fall in line." He didn't mention that he'd had to because Andreas Martin Del Marco hadn't taken the fact that his only son was gay well. He hadn't screamed, raged, or threatened to end his life, which had happened to other people Sebastian knew, but the warm, loving father who'd doted on his son was gone, replaced by a cold and distant stranger.

Sebastian missed the father who had held him, who had told him almost daily how proud he was of him in his strong Puerto Rican accent, who had pushed him hard but cheered him on. Sebastian had to prove he was still a man regardless of who he loved, so he had served, and not just two years but six.

He had earned his father's respect, his acknowledgment, but the love he'd known forever? That hadn't returned, no matter how many honors he received. Glacier sheets layered his family visits, making him cold and shivery. Trips home became rare, buffeted with excuses his mother easily parsed out but had decided to let be.

"I've been all over," he told Red. "I think that's one of the main reasons I enjoy being a traveling nurse. I can go any-where and work."

Red nodded, and Sebastian nearly fangirled when he angled his body toward him to listen more. It was a small victory, but he felt like he'd been running a marathon and had just crossed the finish line. Now, if he could just earn his fantasy prize.

"Where have you been?" Red's hazel eyes sparkled in the fluorescent light.

Do they change color when he's excited?

Sebastian and Red continued chatting until the instructor finished checking over paperwork. Sebastian finally felt better about the class after being nervous over the whole thing. He still wasn't sure about getting a concealed carry license. But ever since he'd been followed to his car one night and had told his girlfriends, Mavis and Cassandra, about it, both kept insisting he should get the license. Mavis and Cassandra were polar opposites, but they had formed a united storm front, believing he needed to be prepared to protect himself.

Sebastian had tried to argue that he knew hand-to-hand combat, having trained in the military, but he hadn't been able to convince them or even himself. So here he was, about to sit through an eight-hour class, babbling away, as usual, dazzled by a man who gave him a hard-on just by sitting beside him.

Though he was ready for the long haul, it was nice to know he'd spend it next to the eye candy that was Gentry *Red* Redmond.

CHAPTER TWO

How long is this manual anyway?

Red flipped through a few of the pages. He'd known the class was going to last forever, but damned if his beast wasn't getting worse the longer the instructor droned on. Something had it on edge, and ignoring it was becoming a problem. He could all but feel the tips of his wings unfurling in his mind. Wouldn't take much for them to explode from his back, stretched and ready for flight.

Fuck. Red had canceled a visit with his family the other weekend. Now he was paying the price with a thin veil of control over his beast. He could have gone home, flown, but he'd chosen drinks with some guys at work. A quick lay. Hell, he thought he'd settled himself down a bit, but this was going to be an issue for him and those around if he didn't figure out what had his griffin so anxious.

He decided to head home the coming weekend and meet up with his brother, Jacobi, who had promised some neighbors his help building a barn. Then he would work around the farm, make himself useful, and wear his beast out. The more he contained himself, the harder it was to live as a human. He and his griffin needed an outlet.

He sighed when the same voice spoke up again, followed by collective groans from the rest of the class.

More questions?

The lady in the back had some doozies. Hell, she'd worried him from the first when she didn't know whether she was carrying an automatic or a revolver. From the sound of it, she hadn't hit anything on her target in the initial qualification, either. She'd even left her bullets on a table outside and walked away. And that was just after the instructor had told them to put their belongings in their vehicles and to know where their ammo was at all times.

That woman didn't need a gun, even if she had served in the military a hundred years ago.

As for the military, it had been a surprise to learn Flirty was in the reserves after serving six years. Of course, that alone got his attention, but then there was everything the man said that just continued to surprise Red. And shooting? Flirty was a good shot and apparently knew what he was doing with a weapon. Surprisingly, Red had caught himself staring at Flirty's ass in those tighter than hell jeans more than a few times, too.

Red had to admit he was glad to be sitting next to Flirty. The man was interesting and funny, and he made him laugh. Before he knew it, he was looking forward to the pauses in the lesson when Flirty took a moment to talk to him, focus drifting over Red's body as he spoke. Red hadn't missed Flirty's extra perusal, which had his beast preening at the attention.

And Flirty touched him—a lot. At first, he thought it was intentional, some way to try and draw him to the *Gay Side*, but the more he watched Flirty, the more he realized the guy was just open and free. Flirty turned to listen to the kid next to him, and he saw Flirty touch the kid's shoulder, then laugh.

He felt it then, a slow burn, nothing overly noticeable but enough to make him aware that neither he nor his beast were fans of bed-hair boy getting Flirty's attention. And that got his mind whirling.

It also got him up and taking a walk, getting his head on straight because his beast's awareness was becoming more forceful. It liked the way Flirty smelled, and it wanted to be closer. The interaction with the bed-hair boy was just the encouragement he needed to find some space, some distance, and pull himself away from the light that was drawing him in—he Icarus, and Flirty the sun.

When he returned, it was finally time for lunch. He thought Flirty would use this as a moment to grab something, but instead, he heard him talking on the phone, making plans to have Thai for dinner. Thai? He knew a few people who liked it, but if he was going to eat something that might as well be Chinese to him, he'd just as soon order from Double Dragon and get some chicken and broccoli.

He got in his truck and tried hard not to wonder why he kept thinking about the man he left behind.

Sebastian watched with disappointment as Red left. They'd made a sort of connection, Sebastian thought. But before he knew it, Red stood and walked out of the room. Maybe it was sharing the same space for hours now. Or having the door shut and surrounded by people, like sardine-wrapped and sealed in a throwaway can? Oh, and the questions coming from the peanut gallery? Yeah, that was enough to drive someone a little crazy, even a person who seemed as well put together as Red.

When Red returned, Sebastian tried speaking to him, but a wall was suddenly between them. Shrugging it off, Sebastian walked out of the room along with the others who went to hurry for food to bring back as requested. Instead of following the group outside, he leaned against a storefront counter and called Mavis.

"Hey, doll, are we still on for tonight?"

"As far as I know. I just have a few things to wrap up, and I can be there around six. Is that good?"

Mavis sounded stressed, and he would generally ask her

about that, but his attention was drawn to tree trunk thighs and a ball cap. And boots. Nice boots.

"Yes." He sighed as he watched Red stride purposefully through the store, boots thudding across the tile and out the door.

"Sebby, what was that sigh about?"

Mavis's tone held a distinct smile, and Sebastian tried his best to ignore it. She had a way of wheedling information out of him if he wasn't careful.

"What sigh?" he asked instead.

"The longing one, like you just lost your puppy. The one you just made a few seconds ago."

He could almost see her lining up, pulling her glasses down to peer over the edges and snaring him with a look.

"I don't know what you're talking about." He moved forward a bit so he could see Red walking to a truck that must have cost a small fortune with all the flash attached to it. Mmm . . . and the man looked good behind the wheel, holding the reins of that monster. Ready to do some damage.

Sebastian did a little shimmy to help relieve the pressure on his hardening cock.

"There. You did it again."

Sebastian shook his head and turned away, visions of cowboy in his head. "Did what again?"

"Ugh. Are you even listening to me? What were you looking at just now?"

Sebastian thought about Red. He refused to say his name and attach any importance to him. Mavis would hear it — the woman could pick shells from a beach shore during a tsunami. "One of the students in the class."

"Oh, no, honey. Don't try to fool me. I heard that sigh. That was you drooling over one of the students in the class. Who is he? Tell me about him." Mavis was digging in now, ready to grill Sebastian, all his secrets filleted open and raw for her to see. "It's been so long since you—"

"No, it's not like that." Nope, they were so not going there.

"It is so like that. Anyway, we can talk tonight."

Sebastian just groaned. "Yes, okay. Look, I'm going to go in and sit. We're on break, and I brought a light snack, so I'd be ready to fill up on our faves." He tore open his granola bar and took a bite, then drank some of his water to wash it down.

"Good. I will be appeased for now, but I want to hear later. How's the class?"

"Pretty good. The teacher is an older guy, like someone's favorite uncle. Has all these stories to tell, which makes the time go by faster, maybe not fast enough, but yeah. And I've gotten to know quite a few of the participants." He'd even exchanged a number with a couple of them who wanted advice for one ailment or another or just to keep in touch.

Mavis laughed, the sound like tiny wind chimes in the wind. "I would expect nothing less."

She always teased him about how quickly he drew a crowd. Could he help it, and why would he want it to stop? He enjoyed people and had found a profession that allowed him to help others. So his contact list took him ages to page through? That was fine.

"Oh, shut up, girl. I'm going back." Sebastian would finish the rest of his snack to tide him over until dinner later.

"Okay, thanks for doing this, Sebastian. I know you didn't want to." The touch of sympathy in her tone was sweet, but the evident rod of steel said she wasn't backing down, either.

He got it.

"No, I didn't, but I understand. Okay, going. See you tonight." They blew kisses over the phone, then hung up.

It wasn't long before the other participants returned. Sebastian was fooling himself if he didn't admit he was looking for Red, who hadn't shown up with the others. Shaking his head, he turned back to answer a question from Corey, who had placed a hand on the back of Sebastian's chair. Corey was nice enough, and from the way the kid had been checking him out, growing more confident with it, he knew he could find a place to get rid of some of his *urges* if he wanted.

A throat cleared, and Sebastian looked up to see if the teacher was signaling them to begin. Instead of the grizzly-haired teacher, though, it was Red.

"Hey," Sebastian said. Was he drooling? He hoped he wasn't, but he could see where it might be a possibility. The man was beautiful, redwood tree tall with arms like branches that he had an overwhelming urge to climb.

"Hey," Red replied and put his things on the table.

"How was lunch?"

CHAPTER THREE

There were so many ways Red could answer that. He could say it sucked because he didn't have a chatterbox next to him. Or that Double Dragon was too far, so he'd dropped by a closer Chinese restaurant instead and would probably hate himself later. He could even say he'd missed Flirty, which would be just plain crazy.

Missing a person I've only just met? What kind of sense does that make?

"Good. You?"

"Oh, I just ate a granola bar. I plan to go to dinner with a friend when I leave here. There's a Thai restaurant in Saint Matthews that I love. It's called Simply Thai, and they just opened a new one in Middletown. Have you been there?"

Red settled in with Flirty's voice curling over him as the firmly muscled sparkling ball of energy told him about why he loved Thai and the different places he'd tried. Red could see the college boy angling in to talk, but no, Red wasn't feeling charitable right now. He was still here for the next four hours, hours he would never get back. He'd had a horrible lunch, and the only good thing about any of this day was the guy sitting next to him. A man with a light in his eyes that made him warm and a laugh that danced over him, tickling his senses.

He sent the college boy a look the kid should have no trouble understanding. He pushed a bit of his energy into the glare, enjoying how the pulses rose and fell. He liked the way college boy responded by quickly abandoning all attempts of speaking to Flirty, leaving him able to sit back and listen. Yeah, he was a little possessive, but it wasn't in his kind to back down. Right now, for whatever reason, he needed to be the center of Flirty's world. That was what mattered to him.

"No," he answered. "I've never eaten Thai before."

"Wow, really? You've been missing out."

The schoolteacher next to them asked Flirty about one of the Simply Thai restaurants.

Flirty happily nodded. "I've been to every one of them. That one is good, probably the best, but there's a new one that I've been waiting to try. So that's where I'm going tonight. It's a better location. Same family, just a different part of Louisville. I'm looking forward to it."

Yeah, Red had heard part of Flirty's conversation regarding going out to dinner. But he was still struggling with the idea of how he felt about that. Was Flirty going on a date, or was it a friend thing? And why did he find himself caring what Flirty did?

Then Flirty focused on him again, and his beast cheerfully soaked up the attention. Red listened as Flirty described the restaurants he'd already visited as well as his favorite dishes. The way he spoke and the sunny look in his eyes did nothing to stop the feeling growing within Red. The pleasure of having the man's gaze wandering over him again, the way his hand would touch him here or there, little flutters of delight following each. Instead of Red drawing back or moving away, he found himself leaning into the warmth of Flirty. Before he could question his movements, the threat of the most boring videos in hell became a terrible reality, a two-hour-long reading of gun laws.

As the end of the class neared, the instructor started the review for the final test, and Red could practically feel the tension in the room. He wouldn't be surprised if the room echoed with applause once everyone was released and able to continue their lives. Hell, he was more than ready for the class to be over. But for some reason, he wasn't quite ready to leave Sebastian.

Sebastian glanced around while taking the test that would be his ticket to freedom. Being here for eight hours hadn't been horrible. But of course, he was one of those people who always looked on the bright side. He'd made a few friends here, and talking to Red had been the highlight of his day. Seeing the man's wariness leave his face and be replaced with warmth reminded him of how lonely he'd been lately. But he wasn't crazy. The man was straight, and it was better not to be foolish thinking something could develop between them, no matter how much he wanted that.

Besides, it's not like we'll ever see each other again.

And how many times have I let myself feel something only to have it fail?

The instructor scored each test as they were handed in, so Sebastian and the others learned they'd all passed. Even the woman in the back who worried him and the guy who was always one or two statements behind and highly concerned with taking guns across states. He'd remember them later when they showed up on the six o'clock news or turned out to be one of the feature stories on his news app.

He gathered his things and headed out, eager to call Mavis and tell her that he was getting ready to go, only to hear she wouldn't be going after all.

"What? Oh, come on." Without realizing it, he spoke in both Spanish and English, which Mavis had no problem following.

It was one of the first things they'd learned about each other when they met in college. Sebastian had been so hurt and angry when he discovered the guy he'd been dating was seeing someone else and that the *girlfriend* hadn't known about them. He'd read Bryan the riot act in a class they had together. When Bryan and his perky little blonde thing left, Mavis had been there, asking if he was okay. She'd spoken in Spanish while gazing around, checking for listening ears. He'd sighed and nodded. Then the two of them had gone for coffee. They had been friends ever since.

And now she was canceling on him.

"Oh, come on, Sebby," Mavis pleaded. "I'm sorry. I truly thought I would be able to get out of here in time, but someone just dropped another set of folders on my desk, and the lawyer's case moved up. I can't go. You know I would."

"Yes, chica, I know, but I really wanted to try it. It's a new one," Sebastian almost whined.

Mavis had promised, but then she had to work, and Sebastian had to understand. That was what friends did, but he didn't like it.

He already knew Cassandra wouldn't be able to escape her gruesome twosome. He loved Cassie and her little rugrats with all his heart and would be visiting them as soon as he got a chance, because he adored hearing them call him Uncle Sebby. He could only hope for some private time to chat with Cassie and catch up. At least he could get that with Mavis . . . or would have.

Well, I could go alone, but —

"I'll go," a familiar whiskey-strong voice said behind him.

Confident the surprise showed clearly on his face, he still turned to its source. Red appeared just as surprised as Sebastian, if his deer in headlights expression was anything to go by.

"I'm sorry," Sebastian said. "What did you say?" He had to ask, right? There was no possible way he'd just heard what he thought he had.

"I'll go with you to the Thai restaurant."

And there it was. Sebastian worked on controlling his

breathing. Passing out right here in the middle of the gun store was not an option, no matter that the future focus of his wet dreams had asked him out.

"Sebastian, who's that? What's going on? And that voice. God, I'm going in heat just hearing it come through the phone. Sebastian?" Mavis called out.

But Sebastian could only stare at Red, who apparently waited for him to answer, arms folded, biceps as big as melons. The need to touch and test their firmness proved challenging to ignore, and Sebastian's dick hardened in response.

"Uhm, Mavis, I'll talk to you later. Looks like I have a partner to try out the new restaurant tonight after all."

Mavis was still chattering, but he ignored it and hung up. She would just have to forgive him later.

He cleared his throat. "So, okay? Tonight?"

"That's when you wanted to go, right?" Red stepped closer, his broad frame moving into Sebastian's space.

Sebastian so wanted Red's nearness, but it was vital for him to remember Red was straight, that Red wasn't coming on to him. What Sebastian refused to be was one of those gays who tried to make a straight boy come to the wild side only to break his own heart. He'd seen it happen, and fuck, he'd nearly done it to himself. Experimenting in college had almost broken him. He wasn't taking another trip on that roller coaster. He'd tried trusting in relationships before. He was always too much or not enough.

He felt his phone buzz once, twice, and then stop. He'd listen to the voicemail later and read the text coming through when he could. Red was the only person he wanted to speak to right then.

Sebastian nodded, dazed by bright hazel eyes and lush pink lips. "Well, yes," he croaked.

Red smelled so good, smoky, and delicious, like something good enough to eat.

"What time?" This time Red was even closer.

Sebastian could feel the heat coming from the man and licked his lips. "Are you sure? We just met, have only been sitting here for like ever. You don't have—"

"I know what I don't have to do."

They were standing outside the classroom door, surrounded by display shelves and comfortable black leather couches. The army-green aesthetic made everyone look pale and almost sickly. Not Red, though—he glowed as if he carried his very own spotlight. A few people from the class were still milling around, but Red was focused on him, and he remained lost in the heat of Red's gaze, as if Red was a newly discovered planet and Sebastian his satellite, orbiting around him for as long as he was permitted.

And that wasn't the only thing Sebastian wanted. Touching. He wanted some touching involved. Better than that? Fucking. Fucking would be lovely.

Red was solid and had the longest legs that Sebastian wanted wrapped around him. He also had the most gorgeous eyes Sebastian had ever seen, and he'd seen a lot of them.

Right now, those eyes were staring at him, waiting.

CHAPTER FOUR

Red had no idea what made him volunteer to go with Flirty. He didn't want to admit he'd been listening to Flirty talk, but he had. When he'd heard Flirty's disappointment about his friend not being able to meet him at the restaurant, the offer blurted out of his mouth before he could clamp it down. So now his body nearly covered the man in front of him, waiting to hear his response, willing him to say yes. There was no way he was going to accept no.

"Okay, sure." Flirty's response seemed unsure.

Relief flushed out the sudden strange jealousy and possessiveness he felt toward Flirty. He was fine with everyone loving whoever they wanted and all of that, but it had always been women for him. When he found the mate his family determined was out there, she would be a woman. Right?

Right now, though, the only person he wanted to be near was Flirty. His griffin was completely on board.

"So, I was planning on driving over there now. Are you ready?" Sebastian asked, his gaze darting around the room and back to Red.

"Yes," Red responded.

Red moved forward without thought, stepping into Flirty's space only to have Flirty step back a little in retreat. He couldn't help himself . . . he stepped closer. Flirty was triggering something inside him, flipping some type of switch. Flirty's scent, the way it wrapped itself around him and teased his senses, was irresistible. Vanilla and cinnamon. Hints of smoked hickory. He wanted more. Wanted to slide himself along Flirty's skin and steal a taste. Predator and prey.

"Uhm, okay." Flirty swallowed deeply.

Red's heartbeat sped up. He made Flirty nervous, stopping him from talking, which was a fantastic accomplishment, as he'd thought the man would never shut up. Or at least that was what he wanted in the beginning. Now, he wasn't so sure.

"So, you want to ride with me?" Red liked the idea of Flirty in his truck, of taking care of him.

Flirty slowly blinked as if trying hard to focus on something. "I'll drive. I drove here. I'll give you the name, and we can meet there." He licked his lips.

Red glimpsed his tongue's quick path and the curve of its movement before Flirty told him the address for the restaurant.

Nodding, Red smiled and forced himself to walk away and out of the store, heading to his truck, directions from the GPS on the phone ready.

Sebastian watched Red go, enjoyed the view, and groaned. He was in trouble. Yes, Red had talked to him, would probably have kept talking to him. He'd been fun to sit next to, to enjoy while they were in the class, both of their asses going numb, or maybe just Sebastian's. But a date?

Well, it isn't truly a date, is it?

Red felt sorry for him and had simply offered to go. Sebastian was stunned, but he wasn't going to forfeit a chance to sit across from Captain America. He wasn't stupid.

He walked out to his car—Red's truck already gone—and got in.

When he arrived at Simply Thai, cars filled the parking lot for miles. Maybe this hadn't been a good idea. He could have just begged off, told Mavis he'd meet her next week. They wouldn't be able to go tomorrow, because it was closed on

Sundays, but maybe when he returned from Florida?

When he looked up after finally finding a space, he noticed he wasn't that far from Red's giant truck. He'd seen the behemoth parked outside the store, had watched Red's superb glutes roll in his jeans as he climbed in. He was a fan of men who knew how to wear pants that showcased a great ass, and Red certainly had one. He shook himself. This wasn't a date. He wasn't going to have a chance to squeeze that luscious ass no matter how much he wanted to.

Red waved at him, and Sebastian took a deep breath. He trembled, creating his own six-point-zero earthquake. Shit, if he didn't know better, he would think he'd suddenly developed asthma, the way his heart was racing. Maybe it was a panic attack. Telling himself he was silly, that this was just Red being kind, he exited the car, but that didn't stop his hands from sweating, just a little.

Red saw when Flirty drove up in a sweet little Lexus, if a person liked that sort of thing. He enjoyed trucks, always had. Trucks were dependable, got a person where they needed to go with the ability to move their stuff along with them. But a sedan? Not for him.

When Flirty finally got out of the car, Red stopped thinking about what the man drove and just watched him. There was a chill in the air, so Flirty had on a peacoat over his bedazzled dragon wings t-shirt, buttoned up to his neck.

When he neared him, Red asked, "Cold?"

"Well, yes. Not all of us are built like bears." Flirty shivered, then his eyes widened, obviously surprised at his own words.

Red laughed, shaking his head. "Come on, then. Let's get you in there and warm." He stood back to let Flirty go in front of him. "I called ahead to get us a table."

"You did?"

Red loved that look of shock on Flirty's face, the way his brows rose as he stared back at him.

"Yeah, a new place is probably going to have a lot of people trying to eat there, and if this type of food is as good as you say it is, it would be difficult to get us a seat."

Flirty nodded, and the way he looked at Red made his chest double in size. Then, proud he'd done something to earn that look, he opened the door for him. Flirty tossed him a sideways glance before stepping forward.

Not a date. Red had to keep reminding himself. This was just dinner with a friend, but Flirty wasn't a friend. Flirty was a guy he'd met at a gun class and then invited himself to share a meal with. A man he now sat across from after helping him out of his coat, breathing in his scent.

What. The. Ever-loving. Fuck.

Red shook his head but waited as Flirty settled back, apparently more comfortable now. Flirty's words began to flow. He informed Red of the several types of curry, the heat levels, and which ones would be savory or not.

Flirty obviously loved his Thai, his hands talking as much as his mouth, a smile on his face as he shared his opinions on which items on the menu Red might like. And Red wore a smile of his own, just enjoying the tsunami of energy that was Flirty. He admired the light reflecting in his hair and the way his eyes seemed to glow when he spoke.

Red was a sun creature, and Flirty's illumination drew him. Being near him was like basking in the sun's rays. He was irresistible.

"Sebastian?"

It was the first time Red had used his name, and he liked the way it rolled off his tongue. Apparently, Sebastian hearing his name was enough for the man to pause in the middle of his lessons on Thai cuisine.

"Yes."

"How about you order for me, okay? I like what I hear, like you telling me about it, but this is new to me, so I'm going to trust you to give me something good." He leaned forward and felt his energy slide across the table around the glasses and lick at Sebastian's aura.

Sebastian's brown eyes blazed much richer in the light, the deep brown hypnotic. "You'd let me order for you?"

Red felt the warmth radiating from Sebastian, the excitement, and it drew him in further. "Why not? You know more about this place than I do. Even if it's new to you, the food isn't. Go for it."

Sebastian's Adam's apple bobbed, and Red wondered what it would be like to nibble the skin there. Instead, he sipped his water, watching Sebastian closely.

"Oh, okay. Uhm." Sebastian stumbled over his words, his brows creased, and he quickly looked back to the menu, his tongue sweeping out again.

Red finally settled back and took another sip of his water, his dick stretching beneath the zipper of his jeans.

While Sebastian studied the menu, occasionally glancing up, Red looked around the restaurant. It was nice, as places like this went, and he supposed they achieved their intent. The large seats were roomy, the décor like something from another country. The dark hues and tones of wine and dark browns and blues blended with gold enhanced the atmosphere. There were long benches, tables, and a few corners just for two. The lighting was dim but not quite dark. The gold accents on the walls gave the place a sort of glow he could appreciate. The thick wood of the table he and Sebastian were sharing was comfortable, but the idea of sitting in one of those corner booths played in his mind. He liked the thought of that privacy.

When the waiter arrived, Sebastian rambled off a list of things Red knew nothing about—curries and some type of puffs. The waiter's head bobbed as he wrote down each one, making sure he asked about the heat level. Red was good with spicy, but too spicy sometimes ruined the food. So he went with a level three, his only contribution to the order.

"Well, I think you'll love it. I do. I've been to the other one in Saint Matthews, but when they said they were opening this location here in Middletown, I had to try it." Eager Sebastian was back again.

Red tuned in, smiling and breathing in vanilla and cinnamon. *Hungry.* "I can tell you've been looking forward to it. Could hear it in your voice on the phone."

Well, that did it. Sebastian would now know for sure that he'd been eavesdropping, but that wasn't exactly new information. That was how they ended up here, and looking at Sebastian across from him, here was precisely where Red wanted to be.

They chatted as they waited for the food, Sebastian, of course, talking the most, hands all over the place.

"You talk a lot," Red said.

Instead of that shocking Sebastian into silence, though, he simply laughed. "Guilty as charged. I'm just naturally interested in people around me, in learning about them. It makes my job easier. The more I talk, the more my patient knows, and that makes them comfortable with me." He shrugged nonchalantly. "It works. But do feel free to jump in whenever you want. I would love to learn more about you."

"You mean, you don't know everything already? You asked me enough questions today." Red stretched out his legs, placing one against Sebastian's.

Sebastian's cheeks reddened, but the smile that followed was stunning rather than shy. "Yes, I did. Doesn't mean that you don't have more to give, so share. What do you do? What are you interested in? Siblings?"

Chapter Five

Sebastian leaned forward to hear Red's response, his heart stuttering over the man's slow smile. He could see himself enjoying the way Red's smile hit his eyes often, basking in their glow. Red just had a relaxed way about him, something that seemed to calm Sebastian.

Sebastian's natural speed was Mach one, with work and his friends. He just didn't have the time to stop and inhale the scent of the proverbial roses or a walk through the park. Instead, time often swallowed him up like a mudslide in the hills of California.

The way Red commanded the space around him, taking his time, said he was well aware of his power and wouldn't be rushed.

Sebastian liked it.

"I'm an architect at the Estopinal Group LLC," Red explained.

Sebastian nodded, even though he didn't know anything about the company. He was based here, but he was a traveling nurse. It didn't allow him time to learn the local businesses, which would be nearly impossible in a city as large as Louisville.

"Building and designing. How long have you been there? Are you happy?" That was what truly mattered to Sebastian. Sure, a person could make all the money in the world, but if he wasn't happy at his job, what was the point of going?

"Well, I interned there my last year of college and was pretty much hired right out."

"So, you're good at what you do. I'm not surprised." And he truly wasn't. Red just looked like a man that had his shit together, someone who wouldn't be afraid to take risks and come out shining in the end. He admired that, along with a few other things he would do his best not to focus on.

Sebastian nodded and turned to the waiter, who had just arrived with help, because all the items he had ordered needed a caravan to carry to their table. "Oh, it smells so good. God, I could live off the scent alone." He inhaled deeply as they placed the hot and savory dishes down, making room for the small buffet.

"Ahh, you're right about that. It certainly smells good." Red's mouth watered a little in anticipation as he and Sebastian dug in.

The food tasted good, too. Red had to admit that the curry puffs with the cucumber dipping sauce won him over instantly. But his favorite was the pineapple curry that slid over his tongue, leaving a trail of sweetly tempered heat. He groaned with pleasure as he finished off the last of it, tempted to pick up his plate and lick the dregs of it away.

When he looked up, Sebastian was staring at him with barely veiled interest, his lips opened wide.

"Uhm." Sebastian's smoky topaz eyes lowered as he cleared his throat and suddenly busied himself with the dish he was enjoying. "Sounds like you enjoyed that one."

Red would have to be deaf to miss the hunger in Sebastian's tone. Plus, the aroma of the man's desire gave him away.

"Oh, yeah. That was fucking good." Red happily groaned as he savored his meal and Sebastian's lust.

He'd never been interested in a man before, or at least not any time he could remember. For some reason, Sebastian felt different. Hell, the whole inviting himself to dinner with the man was a new thing for him, and he was trying real hard not to question his actions.

He wanted what he wanted, and at the moment, what he desired most was to be around Sebastian, hear his laugh and have a little more of his light wrapped around his soul.

Looking around the restaurant, he wondered if anyone here thought the two of them were on a date. There were several couples, a few families, and a couple of loners. The lighting was dim, like restaurants did to create an ambiance. But hell, he would be hard-pressed to deny that this was a date in his mind. And it wasn't like he'd be disappointed if they did. He didn't know why, but he was feeling possessive. His kind often did with anything they deemed theirs. And while Sebastian wasn't a woman, there was something about him that called to his griffin, pushing him to lean closer, to nibble and taste, to drink in Sebastian's scent. He couldn't resist breathing deep, enjoying the hints of cinnamon and vanilla he'd noticed earlier.

He took another bite of his food, humming to himself. The flavors burst on his tongue, sweet pineapple and spicy curry. Tender carrots and peppers blended with onions. The steak was seasoned well and reminded him of something he'd enjoyed at his mother's table. He groaned in pleasure.

When he opened his eyes, he fell into the chocolate depths of Sebastian's gaze. He liked it there.

Fucking good was absolutely the words Sebastian would have used. Seeing Red dive into his pineapple curry with gusto, sighing at the aroma when he poured it over his brown rice, made Sebastian's dick take notice. It pressed against his zipper, searching for a path to freedom, eager to acquire some of those yum-yum noises coming out of Red's throat. He'd considered button-fly jeans that morning and was so glad he changed his mind. The buttons would have malfunctioned, unable to hold back the monster trying to hulk its way out of his underwear.

When Red had finished his pineapple curry and licked his lips, he'd popped a thumb into his mouth to gather whatever he could find there. Sebastian swore to himself, knowing he could come from that visual alone. Oh, he was in so much trouble. Then Red had looked at him, and Sebastian knew he couldn't hide how much he wanted him, but he had to keep things casual. *Remember this is not a date.*

"Good, I'm glad you're enjoying the meal." Sebastian shuddered, thinking if Red sounded that good when he enjoyed his food, sex had to be a spectacular event, complete with pleasured hums and sighs of gratification.

He cleared his throat. "So, let's see what else we have that you may want to try."

They made it through most of the dishes, but both had to wave the white flag at the last one. Since it was Red's first time, Sebastian decided he would sacrifice and allow Red to take the leftovers with him.

The bill arrived, and before Sebastian could swipe it off the table, it was in Red's hand, his fingers clasped around the edges.

"I was going to pay," Sebastian said.

Red reached back and pulled out his wallet. "No, my treat."

"Well, I could pay half." He'd intended to pay for Mavis. He could do the same for Red.

"Nope. I had fun tonight. It was worth it." Red smiled at him, his gaze intense.

Sebastian's skin warmed with the way Red's gaze slowly traveled over him. He turned away, clearing his throat again, and waited for the server to return.

When they were all packed up and heading to their vehicles, Red stopped him with a touch to his arm, which was far warmer than anything Sebastian's coat could provide. Sebastian turned back to face him before entering his car.

"Maybe we can do this again sometime?" Red asked.

The look on Red's face was calm, but Sebastian could see the tell-tale signs that he was anything but. For some reason, Red wanted more, and Sebastian didn't know what to do with that.

"Again?" Sebastian swallowed. He'd been telling himself repeatedly this wasn't a date, that he was setting himself up for an emotional mudslide. He needed to stop this and pull himself back from the edge.

"Yeah, I had fun. You did, too. Why not?" Red stepped closer, nearly pressing himself against Sebastian.

"Yes, I had fun." Sebastian sighed as he breathed in Red's spicy scent. It wasn't a cologne he recognized, but he was sure he would never forget it. The way it flowed over him in waves caused everything around them to disappear.

"I need your number," Red said as he leaned closer. "Let's have fun again."

"Red, you know I'm gay, right?" Sebastian had to ask, even though his voice came out in a husky whisper rough enough to sand paint.

Red had to know what this looked like, with his body all but on top of Sebastian's. He was closer than friends would be, which is the only thing Sebastian thought he could have with this man. Right then, he wasn't sure and didn't know if Red had a clue either.

"Yeah, but what does that have to do with me getting your number?"

Red knew he was standing too close, but he couldn't help himself. He wanted to see Sebastian again, see the way those brown eyes darkened, listen to him talk. He wasn't lying. He'd had fun, and it had been so long since he'd simply let go and enjoy himself.

Sebastian laughed nervously, and Red knew he'd won before realizing how hard he tried for the prize. He stepped back and placed the food on the car, pulling out his phone and setting up a new contact, then handed it to Sebastian, who looked up at him and then back to the phone. He watched as Sebastian entered his number, smiling at the thought of calling him.

When Sebastian finished, he handed back the phone. Red took it, their hands touching. Sebastian gasped, and Red groaned. Yeah, he thought so. There was something . . . something more, and he wanted to find out what.

"You're right. This was fun," Sebastian said, his smile crooked and enticing. "Don't be a stranger."

Red smiled. "Oh, I won't be."

That's a promise.

Then Sebastian was in his little car driving out of the lot, leaving a slightly confused but pleased Red behind.

Before he could think more on their touch or the way Sebastian's scent had almost driven him to taste the man, his phone rang.

Seeing his father's name, he answered. "Sir."

"Need you here at the farm. And while you're here, you can tell me why I felt your energy change." His father's voice crackled over the line, his tone warranting an immediacy Red knew better not to ignore.

"Yes, sir."

CHAPTER SIX

R ed parked in front of the homestead, and even though it wasn't that late, it was already pitch black. He took a deep breath, the desire to take to the air challenging to resist. Instead of stripping and taking advantage of the darkness, the need to feel the breeze beneath his wings, he headed to the wraparound porch his father had built years ago. It was beautiful here, the way the light from the moon cast a glow over the family home. He missed it sometimes, walking along the lake, taking a slow swim. He missed the quiet, gentle sounds of the animals and the scents, missed seeing it all from miles above, floating on the wind. He liked the city, but the space and openness of the family land gave him a calmness like no other.

Still, he came home often enough for the hunts with his father, the moments when they would all take flight except for his mother, who would spell the night, helping them to remain invisible to the watchful eye. But this night wasn't scheduled for a hunt. According to his father, his energy had changed, whatever that meant. He reached to open the door, pausing when the sounds indicated Jacobi was near.

"Hey, Red," Jacobi shouted. "Father says you met your mate. Who is she? What does she look like?"

Jacobi was carrying a crate that would probably have weighed down most humans, the way his muscles strained. That didn't stop his brother from turning his massive frame toward Red, sniffing in his direction trying to catch his fragrance. Jacobi was taller than him, his wingspan magnificent.

But his gift was his nose, the fact that he could detect his prey's trail for miles. The family had put it to use, and Jacobi's ability had only grown over the years. His skill to define every nuance, every characteristic of a target detectable to him alone defied logic.

Jacobi's dark green eyes glowed as he looked at Red, nodding when he'd apparently captured what he sought.

Red froze as Jacobi flashed him a knowing smile.

Mate? Where?

He'd been dating Ashley for a bit, Tammy, too. Neither of them was his mate. He'd sort of given up on the mate thing. The clan was fine with his family's distance for now, but the possibility of a mate for him might change things. And not for the good of those he cared for.

"Well, there's a difference, something spicy, warm-blooded." Jacobi stuck out his tongue as if tasting the air and leaned closer, careful not to drop the crate. "Human. It's mixed in with your scent, little hints mostly." He nodded. "Better you than me." He laughed and continued on his path, hefting the box higher, blond hair just like their mother's catching the light.

Red remained frozen to the spot.

"Gentry, you out there?" his father's voice boomed from inside the home.

"Yes, sir. On my way." Red shook himself and entered, letting the screen door bang behind him.

There was nothing like being home, where the comfort of their nest always pleased him. The smell of baked bread wafted into the room, music with the raspy voice of a man who was down to his last dime played in the background. His father sat at the table, reading over papers. He could always count on normal here, the balance he needed after working where there were none like him.

He wouldn't say he was lonely. He had regular partners for sex, guys he played pool with, rode bikes with, and his own place. He didn't need a mate, someone to screw up the balance he had. Then he thought of Sebastian, and that whole *not needing anyone* went straight to hell.

"How'd the class go?" his father asked.

People thought Red was big until they saw his father and Jacobi. Levi Redmond was huge, his colossal frame built to protect, his quick mind to lead. But years ago, he'd chosen to have a family, and to shelter and love the woman he'd married rather than continue the role of Clan Docent, the guide for the clan's wellbeing. It was a decision many had not been in favor of, especially Laith Baher, the current Ilios. But to resume the position by Lath's side would mean to leave behind Alice Kissinger, and his father would not do that.

Although his father had left the safety of the prominent clan, moved states away, and made a life for his family, it didn't mean that he didn't receive calls long into the night. He could still feel the growth of their people, the bonds that developed like threads in the patterns of life as they formed the vast fabric of connections. He would also still know when the next Ilios would be born, able to feel it in his blood. He was still tied to the clan, but at their refusal to accept the woman he loved, he'd made his choice.

"Good," Red replied. "Should have the certificate in a few weeks, could be four." He picked up a tangerine from the bowl of fruit on the table, piercing the flesh quickly with a claw and peeling it back to enjoy its sweet reward.

"Anything happen while you were there?" His father's hazel eyes — a mirror of his own — stared at him, searching.

"No, just a class." Red didn't mention meeting Sebastian, but he couldn't get the man off his mind. He'd been thinking about him constantly, the way he talked and laughed so freely. And now that he had his number, he'd give him a call, but at this moment, he focused on his father, who still looked at him with searching glances. "The instructor said it wouldn't take long to get all of the paperwork done. Then I'll have the permit."

"Good. Need you armed if what I'm hearing is true."

Red knew his father's fears that the clan would grow tired of the distance between them. Laith was not a good and honorable leader who protected the people, guarding their wisdom as those before him had done. He was greedy and volatile, hateful of any opposition. He hadn't been happy with the arrangement made years ago allowing Red's father to leave the clan, and there was talk of bringing the docent's family in by force.

Though his father kept his distance, his sons did not, especially Jacobi. Many of the clan had left their homes and made new ones here in Louisville. They came for help and received it through Jacobi. Because of his brother, the number of new neighbors was steadily growing.

Those who kept close ties with his father mentioned Laith's desire to rule beyond his time. Cutting the threads that would lead to the birth of a new Ilios would go a long way to ensuring his reign was absolute. Laith believed having the docent under his control would all but guarantee it.

"Yes, sir." Red popped the slices of fruit in his mouth, licking his fingers.

"Need you to keep your human form as much as you can. Shifting into your creature should be your last resort." His father scanned the papers curling on the table.

Red finally noticed the papers were blueprints and maps of their land. "Yes, sir, and when the need becomes unbearable, I'll come home." He understood his father's concerns, but he hadn't had the sensation that ran along the surface of his skin like fire ants in months. He hadn't even realized how much he needed to shift and fly until he'd stepped on his family's property. But he was good, or at least that was what he'd been telling himself, although he'd been thinking earlier it was time.

"Hm. I'll have to accept that you know yourself, but we'd rather you be here where there's room if you're needing it. Now, sit and tell me about the energy I felt." As docent of their clan, his father would know if another thread wove into their family tapestry the moment a bond was introduced. He was the history keeper, the defender, the guardian. But Red was his direct descendant, which made clarity difficult. While docents couldn't clearly see how their own lines would change, they could sense the shifts and stretches. They felt it almost immediately.

"Dad, I haven't felt any energy change, nothing that would warrant your concern. I would have known."

His father sniffed. "Not if you're blind to it yourself. Sometimes the mind has a way of keeping things from us, protecting us. But our bodies? Our need to blend our energy with the person made for us will not be ignored. Think, Gentry. We need to know. If there's any possibility you're going to come into your birthright, we will have to protect you. Laith is waiting for a Docent he can control."

"He won't." Red knew that he was one of the strongest in the line. There was no way he would find himself under the Ilios's thumb. Besides, his future lay in his company's progress with him at the helm. He had no interest in being a baby king detector.

"It doesn't mean he won't try, boy. Laith wants to know when the next leader will be born, to what family, so he can destroy it, all because of a power you are helpless to control? In the past, it was our honor to be chosen as guardians for the clan. Now, they will utilize that power as a tool for genocide. We must remain beneath their radar. Your mother has increased the wards both here and at your home, but if you've found your mate? We need to know, Gentry." His father's brow furrowed, staring as if he could press the seriousness inside Red's skull.

Red understood, but he wasn't worried. Without a mate, there was nothing to worry about, but with one, his whole family would be in danger, for it was only with the bonding of he and his mate that his light could pass through to his mate for all to witness. His father's arrangement would be honored. Still, the chance for a new docent, one the clan could welcome, wouldn't be ignored by Laith. The growling as his father looked back at the blueprints couldn't be missed.

He fell into the chair next to his father, one he'd hewn out of cherry wood years ago. Their need to be surrounded by what was natural was vital to them, so they filled their home with things his father and mother had handcrafted. He and Jacobi had helped when they were old enough.

His mother walked in then, her eyes bright and hopeful. Alice Redmond was still beautiful and always would be. Sure, there were lines in her skin, gentle traces of the happiness she'd shared with his father, but they had only appeared in the last several years. A person seeing her would think of his mother in her early fifties, never suspecting she was nearing one hundred. She wore her white-blond hair pulled back into a braid that fell over her shoulder and her typical apron around her waist. She'd been baking again, and Red couldn't wait to try the bread he smelled warming in the kitchen.

"Your father said you met your mate, Gentry. What does she look like? When can we meet her?"

Red's soul warmed when his mother moved through the room to stand behind his father. She was his champion, his best friend, he didn't know what he'd do without her. It was always terrible to see the letdown in her eyes every time she asked, and he'd said there just wasn't anyone out there that made him feel the way his father did for her.

His father looked up from the papers and immediately opened his arms to her, turning his cheek to allow her kiss when she bent.

"Witch, this is between the boy and me," he grumbled.

"The boy is my son, Docent, as much as he is yours. If our family is finally about to grow, I want to know." She turned sharp eyes on Red and waited. "The girl? Tell us about her."

Red wouldn't hesitate if he even had an inkling of what they were talking about, but he didn't. He'd been in class all day, had dinner with Sebastian, and that was all. He hadn't interacted with any new women, human or otherwise. If there were an opportunity to identify a mate, her presence bypassed his awareness.

"Think, Gentry."

"I can think of no one, Dad. I'm sorry." And he was. He wanted—no, needed someone of his own, but as the years continued and no one made an appearance, no one that would love both him and the beast within, he'd just made his peace. Not everyone needed a mate, no matter what his family believed. His life wouldn't fall apart without one. He'd accepted that. Now, his father thought he'd met his. Red shrugged and picked up a napkin, drying his hands.

His father shook his head, his eyes piercing Red's soul. "It is no matter. Fate would not allow you to miss your mate even if I cannot see her. Is it fair that as Docent, I can tell where the new threads will begin, even the golden ones for the next Ilios, but I am denied clear vision for the threads of my family line?" His father harrumphed but settled when his mother ran her fingers through his curly hair, soothing him.

"Everything happens for a reason," his mother said, kissing his father gently on his temple.

"It is for us to discover it. Come, look at these with me. With new possibilities comes the need for change. I want to build a new home here, one that would house a family and yet give them the privacy needed."

"Dad." Red knew what his father was hoping, but it wasn't

going to happen. True, one day, his slow aging would be a concern, which was why he was currently working on establishing his own company. One where he could remain behind the scenes and out of the human eye but still do what he loved. A home with a family of his own? Not what he'd been planning.

"I know what I felt, Red. It's unbelievable that you have not. Even with this lack of awareness, there are steps to be taken. Now, come look with me. Let's use that degree and the experience you've gained to determine what's best. We must have a way to defend ourselves as well."

Red shifted so he could see the papers. Defense. It was all too much right now. Red had been living on his own for the last several years. He'd grown to love his independence and freedom. What his father wanted? His mother? He wasn't sure he wanted the same. Still, he respected his parents, so he made himself comfortable, studying the blueprints and determining the best way to do as his father asked.

Chapter Seven

Sebastian was tired. Florida had been beautiful, and except for a few storms, he'd loved the warm temperatures and the promise of sun and ocean. He'd spent many nights just walking on the shore, his feet bare and comfortable, but it still hadn't been a vacation. Too many hours were spent at the hospital with him falling asleep in the office, drained.

He was ready to be home, ready to kick back in his apartment, maybe use one of those new bath bombs he'd picked up the other day from the soap specialty shop, Lush. Before he'd fully closed the door, a notification for a new email went off on his phone, and he sighed. Not yet. He'd just got home.

Dropping his bags and turning to lock the door, he pulled his phone out of his pocket and looked.

"Oh, thank goodness." It wasn't work. It was, however, the emailed version of his certificate for his CCDW. The teacher said they would receive it in four to six weeks, sometimes earlier. Three weeks wasn't bad. Now all he had to do was take it to the sheriff's office, which could wait until Monday when he was ready to go out again. He had the whole weekend to himself, and he wasn't going anywhere. He was parking his ass on his favorite couch, the purple plush one with the teal pillows, and wrapping himself in his comfy blanket. He planned to curl up in front of his widescreen plasma television, which he'd spent way too much money on but loved, and watch brainless streamed television shows.

Deciding he could always put his things away later, he

walked down the hall and into his kitchen. Chrome appliances he barely had a chance to use filled the room. He popped open his double-wide refrigerator, grabbing one of the imported beers he'd bought before he left. He didn't indulge often, but after the trip he'd had, complete with the layover from hell, he figured he'd earned it.

Flopping down with a beer in hand, he prepared to watch Sherlock or something that didn't require his brain to operate at total capacity. He toed off his shoes and left them at the edge of the oversized couch, then snatched the multicolored afghan he'd picked up from a market in Charleston, South Carolina. He made himself into a burrito, settling onto his couch that was roomy enough to fall asleep on, which he often did. He could burrow in the pillows and be comfortable for hours.

While he flipped through his options, he thought about the email, which, of course, led to him thinking about Red. He hadn't heard from the man, but he wasn't surprised. Dinner at Simply Thai had felt surreal, almost like a date, and that couldn't be. Red wasn't gay, and Sebastian wasn't interested.

Well, maybe that's a small white lie.

He *was* interested. Who wouldn't be? Red was gorgeous, so tall, and just damn big. He'd imagined those wide biceps beneath his palms, hanging on as Red had his way with him. The visual had certainly helped things progress faster when he'd been alone at night. Okay, daytime, too.

Can I help that I have a pretty healthy sex drive and nowhere to expend the energy?

The crazy thing? He hadn't wanted to expend that energy with anyone other than a man he'd probably never see again.

And as fate would have it, that was precisely when Sebastian's phone rang.

He looked at it first, too surprised to see Red's name on his screen. He answered after the second ring, needing to sound cool. Relaxed. Instead, what popped out of his mouth was a squeaky *hello?* Ugh, he sounded like some teenaged girl who'd been waiting on an invitation to the prom. He shook his head, cleared his throat, and tried again. "Hello." There, that was better, more confident, self-assured, or at least he hoped so.

"Hello, Sebastian. Remember me? Red."

Oh, Sebastian remembered. The minute he heard that voice, his dick rose to attention. He'd only seen the man one day and couldn't get him out of his mind. Red's face would appear in his thoughts at the most inconvenient times. When he was moving a patient. When he was reading through suggestions for another. When he was looking out of a window. There was just something about Red that wouldn't go away. And the most embarrassing of all, his dreams of bronze skin, strong hands tight around his waist, making him cry with passion.

Now Red was on the other end of the line waiting for Sebastian to speak, and Sebastian hadn't said a word for how long? He needed to get himself together.

"Yes, hi."

Red paused as if deciding what to say next. "Got the certificate in the mail today. I figured you got yours, too?"

"Yes, I did, actually." So was that the reason he was getting a call? To see if they both got a certificate? He picked up the remote to turn down the sound of the television. Of course, he could always find out the true identity of the creepy emailer on the show he was watching later, when he wasn't on the phone with Red the eye candy cowboy.

"Okay, good. Look, I want to see you."

The rumble in Red's voice did nothing to stop the need spinning summersaults in Sebastian's chest, making him drop the phone like a ninny.

His hands trembled when he located the phone and placed it against his ear again. He coughed. "So, want to see me?"

Red had spoken like he'd already determined they were going out, making Sebastian nervous. But the sound of Red's voice thrumming across his skin created tiny sparks along the way. He could listen to that voice forever. He'd even fantasized about Red using that voice to make him bend to his will. He shivered.

"Yes. I've been thinking about you, and I want to see you. So let's go out, have dinner or go to a movie. What do you like to do?"

"Red—" Sebastian said, but before he could continue, Red stepped in.

"Did you like talking to me, Sebastian? Being with me?"

Oh, God, did I? Yes. Yes. Yes.

"Of course, I did, but—"

"Then go out with me. It doesn't have to be anything serious. Unless we let it. It's just two friends hanging out." Red's words sounded so innocent, so friendly, yet implied more than maybe he realized.

This was such a mistake. Sebastian could see himself getting attached to Red, wanting more from him than the man was prepared to give. He'd been there before and got burned because sometimes he didn't stay home long enough, or other times, he wanted too much. Sebastian had learned to make do with the physical only. Getting emotionally invested would only cause heartbreak. He needed to remember that.

Fantasizing about a relationship with Red was a terrible idea, so then why were his following words, "Okay, I could do that."

What the fuck am I thinking?

That. Sebastian wanted to *do* Red. His palm met his face, and he groaned tiredly.

"Good. Good. Where do you live?"

"Wait. It's late, and I just got here." Sebastian sat up, tiredness forgotten.

"Oh, where were you?"

46

Something laced beneath Red's question, and Sebastian responded to it naturally as if Red already owned a piece of his soul.

"Out of town. I've been in Florida for a few weeks. Left the day after class. My bags are still at the door, and I just flopped down on my couch." Sebastian looked around him. He was typically a neat person, liked to have everything in order, but he'd just gotten home. He couldn't remember if he'd taken the trash out before his trip. There was just the hint of something fishy coming from the kitchen. No. No, this was not a good idea.

"Let me come over. If you don't want to go out, I could bring you something."

"Red, look . . ." If Sebastian was going to see Red, he needed to be fully aware, ready to protect himself. Right now, it seemed as if he had no defenses where Red was concerned, and that wasn't like him. So he needed to wait, maybe go out later. Besides, he also needed to tidy up, himself included.

"Thai. You love it, and I've eaten there a few times myself now. I'll bring it to you. Let me feed you. Give me your address."

And like a lovesick fool, Sebastian did.

Red heard it in Sebastian's voice and knew the man was thinking of how to say no, but he wouldn't let that happen. When he was sitting at his desk earlier, he'd seen the email notification hover over his screen. He'd been thinking of Sebastian at the time, of how it would be to touch him. It wasn't the first time those thoughts had crossed his mind.

Thoughts of Sebastian had been ever-present for weeks now. How many times had he picked up the phone? He hadn't called him, though. But the overwhelming urge had been killing him. He wanted to be near him, speak to him.

What would I have said anyway?

And friends? What he wanted was more than friends. He knew that. The *just friends* spiel he'd given Sebastian? Fuck that. He wanted to be able to touch him, to see how the man's body felt against his own. Taste him. Whenever. He. Wanted. To.

The more time that went by, the more focused he'd become on having the man beneath him.

The minute the notification came through, it was like he'd been given the go-ahead. He called, and hearing that trembling hello on the line made him hungry, awakening his beast. Need rocketed through him and went all the way to his core, the twisting ball of want monstrous in its size. When Sebastian said he'd just gotten there, Red's first thought was that he'd been on a date, and a hot red spear of jealousy struck hard.

He was helpless against the rage of someone other than him having Sebastian. Power rode along his arms and his legs, the burn of it hitting the center of his belly. And Sebastian was sure to hear it in his voice.

"Be there soon."

It didn't take long for Red to pack things away. Then he called, ordering everything they'd shared before plus another appetizer the woman said was their most popular one.

On his way to the elevator, he passed Carol, who just looked at him. "Leaving so soon, boss?"

"Yes, but I'll be in touch. Call if you need me."

He'd hired Carol years ago, which had been one of the best decisions he'd ever made. Efficient and professional, Carol was the epitome of the perfect assistant. Evidence of her love of superheroes could be seen on the desk covered with Marvel everything, including a few pictures of her dressed in cosplay.

He looked forward to her smile, the way she always had something kind to say. She grounded him and made him laugh as she ensured his days at work went off without a hitch.

One blonde brow rose as she studied him. "You never leave this early, Mr. Redmond. Is everything alright? Can I help?"

Red was so excited to see Sebastian that he almost told her, but how would it look? Here he was, a man racing off to see another man? No, that wouldn't do. Of course, it wasn't like Carol would care about that, but he was still dealing with it all himself. He didn't feel like explaining what even he couldn't grasp.

"No, just something came up. Have to see to it myself."

Apparently, Carol wasn't fooled. Her eyes warmed as she asked, "Do you want to call me afterward, have me add it to our files?"

It was a trap. Red knew it, but he wouldn't break. "No, Carol. Completely personal."

Carol smiled and nodded. "Okay, so I'll see you Monday."

Red tried not to think about the knowing smile Carol wore as he strode to the elevator or the way his heart raced with thoughts of seeing Sebastian again.

Driving to the restaurant first, he picked up the food and headed to Sebastian. The weeks between the first time he'd met his little flirt and now had been filled with him trying to figure out what mate his father meant, but there'd been nothing. Instead, he envisioned Sebastian's face, again and again, remembered his voice and how much he wanted to hear it again. He missed talking with him, the way his hands were an animated accompaniment to their conversation.

Red had even gone on a date, but when the woman's nimble fingers crawled over his body, making it beneath the waistband of his briefs, he'd stopped her. He'd held her wrist gently and shook his head no. That had been odd by itself. He had needs, desires he never hesitated to fill. But apparently, the pretty auburn-haired beauty who had sat in his lap trying her hardest to get to his dick would not satisfy them now. And yes, it had been frustrating the hell out of him trying to figure out why that was. Even her pleas to blow him had done nothing for him.

The way he felt right now, how fucking hard he was, he had a clue what might be the cause, and it was scaring the hell out of him. But instead of running the other way, he was running to Sebastian.

Sebastian looked at the door from his couch, waiting. He'd put away his clothes. Okay, threw them in the washroom and shut the door. He did toss out the trash because there *was* fish in there. What had he been thinking to leave that funkiness behind? He'd sprayed the room with *Febreze* and lit a candle because it couldn't hurt. Now, he stared ahead, waiting for the knock to come.

What would Red think of his place? He loved color, which was evident from the décor of his home. Paintings he'd purchased on trips spread out on his walls, along with a section of squared canvas photos of him, Mavis, and Cassandra on their adventures. Chairs, a chaise, his couch, and a sofa covered the room with blankets and woven throws for each. He liked being comfortable anywhere he went in his home.

He hoped Red would feel the same.

No matter how many times he thought about it, he had no idea how things had turned out this way. Him waiting, not so patiently, legs crossed, fingers twisting, wearing his fourth, maybe fifth set of clothes after searching his walk-in closet for the perfect outfit. He'd finally decided on a powder blue sweater and a pair of soft skinny jeans, comfort being key for him. Dress to impress? No. He wasn't going to do that. This wasn't a date. Red hadn't said it was.

Red. What was the draw there other than being gorgeous

as fucking hell? It had been there the first moment he met him, was there at the restaurant.

Usually, when Sebastian was approached, there was only one thing a guy wanted, and he had no problem making it happen. Fucking was easy. He wasn't stupid and never hesitated at sating his needs. Everyone had them, and no one could blame him for having them, too. But that was as far as it went, as far as he would let it go. He'd tried the relationship thing once or twice and decided it wasn't for him. It wasn't that he didn't dream about having someone to hold at night, someone he could wake up with every morning. But he'd never felt anything beyond a need to get off. Then he was done. With his career and the life he led, he didn't have time for heartache.

Yes, I want more. Need more. But more isn't coming, and I'm not fighting for it anymore.

And now here he sat, watching and waiting for Red to come to him. He'd heard something in Red's voice, something beyond interest. And damn if he wasn't interested in seeing what it was.

When the doorbell rang, Sebastian took a deep breath and stood. He didn't want to seem nervous, but that was probably a hopeless case. He thought about sending one of his girls a text, asking them for some quick advice, but he didn't want either of them thinking this was anything more than what it was, either. Okay, whatever it was. If only he knew himself.

"Hello," Sebastian said as he opened the door.

Red stood there smiling, bags in his hands.

The delicious scents of fabulousness hit Sebastian's nose. "Oh, wow. I had no idea how hungry I was." He reached out to take some of the bags. His nose was a Thai detective, and he could already taste the succulent bits of meat and curry that awaited him, the aroma a lure he couldn't deny.

"Neither did I." Red's voice rumbled the words.

There it was again, that something. Sebastian looked up

just as Red's gaze focused on him, traveling down his body and up again before he swallowed deeply. Sebastian saw it then, the way Red's eyes dilated, the rise and fall of the Red's chest, felt the heat that radiated from him. He almost stepped back, suddenly more nervous than ever, nearly dropping the bags of delicious goodies on the floor.

"Red?"

Red stepped forward, his focus intense, searching for what Sebastian had no idea. He called his name again, and Red stopped, shook his head.

"Are you all right? Do you need anything? I could help you."

CHAPTER EIGHT

Yes, Red needed something, and hell no, he wasn't all right. It turned out his father was right. Red had indeed met his mate. Now, what the hell was he supposed to do about it?

"Red?"

He was an idiot. All this time and he'd missed it. There had been signs, of course, the way he kept focusing on Sebastian, always thinking about the man. Sebastian's scent, the musky heat that he'd been searching for since they parted, teased his senses and made him hunger almost desperately. He needed to taste him, have him, feel his body against his own. He wanted Sebastian, the little flirt that had captured him, and he would never let go.

Red walked forward, the beast rising to the surface at the possibility of claiming its mate. He felt the itching along his spine, the crawling sensation on his fingertips. After so many years of waiting, before him stood the one he'd given up hope of ever knowing. The person who would unlock his light, gift him with his sight, allowing him to feel and know the lifelines of his people.

But he couldn't. This wasn't the place or the time. He saw the heat in Sebastian's eyes, but he also saw the fear, the confusion, and he wouldn't add to it, not right now. He wouldn't make his mate prey. Instead, he would take his time and reel him in slowly.

Red took deep breaths, pulled back the beast, slowed his racing heart, and breathed in the calming scent of his mate.

My mate.

"Red, I can help? I'm a nurse, remember? What's going on? How do you feel?" Sebastian was using his nurse voice, the one he'd probably perfected to help those in his care. Soothing and patient.

The sound just made Red harder and drove his desire higher. He wanted to hear Sebastian cry with the need to come, to feel him tremble with desperation, see him fly apart.

I could strip the clothes from your body and make you mine.

"Come over and sit down. I'll get you some water. Let me check your pulse." Sebastian put the bags he held down and left, presumably to get the water.

The refreshing liquid would do nothing for the burning going on inside Red.

Would Red be able to stand Sebastian's touch now that he knew what it could do to him? Would he be able to rein in the fierce need coursing through his body? Or would the power assail Sebastian, enflaming them both?

Before he could think to stop him, his flirt was back, and Sebastian's hand was on his body again. Sebastian gasped as energy sparked between them. His eyes widened, the brown almost molten, his tanned skin taking on a golden hue as rays of light tore out of Red and into Sebastian.

And then it was too late. Red was on him, his skin tingling as he pressed his mouth over Sebastian's, a slave to the need within. So much feeling, so much heat. He groaned, enjoying the pleasure of having his mate tear at him, reaching for his clothes, pulling at his hair.

"I . . . Oh, God. What? I . . ." Sebastian's words were unintelligible as he was lifted from the floor.

Red carried him to a couch off to the side, sitting before a window leading out to a balcony. It got dark so fast during this time of the year, Red could almost see the moon, but he could care less about its glow. It was all about the gift he held in his hands.

"It's our mating. I had no idea, Sebastian, and I can't wait any longer." Red dropped Sebastian next to him, his cock stretching in the prison of his pants as his mind blazed with the thought of taking his mate. He watched a dazed Sebastian writhe in need, touching himself as he tried to calm the same fire that burned within Red. "I never knew my mate could be a man. Would never have thought it, but I can see it, see how you would be what I needed." He shrugged out of his shirt, the fabric sliding down his arms.

"What are you talking about? What is going on with me? Am I drugged? Oh. Fuck. I need you to fuck me. Shit! Where is this coming from?" Sebastian groaned, then slid his sweats down until he could capture his dick in his hand, palming the pink head in his fist.

Red's chest rumbled as the scent of Sebastian's desire washed over him. Freed from his shirt, he fell to his knees and took that swollen head into his mouth, dragging Sebastian's hips closer and swallowing him deep.

His mate's taste slid over his tongue as he whipped it over the round tip, elongating the muscle and wrapping it around Sebastian's hard dick. *Delicious.*

"Oh . . . What . . . What is that? Red?"

Sebastian's cries of pleasure rocked Red to his core. He wanted more, planned to hear his mate lose his mind. He sucked harder, taking more of Sebastian in until he was at his balls and able to breathe him in, feel the tickle of Sebastian's crotch hair against his lips.

Sebastian screamed, and Red's hands became claws, his beast eager to join with Sebastian. He trapped him, holding him securely, not allowing him any other movement than what he gave. He increased the suction when Sebastian tried to move, but he'd caught his prize and wasn't letting go.

"I've never. Oh, my. Ugh." Sebastian released.

And it tasted of ambrosia. The seed rushed down Red's waiting throat, embedding Sebastian's essence into the capillaries of his body, taking his mate's signature and making it a part of his own. Sebastian trembled as thought his body was a sacrifice to the orgasm that was rending him apart, surrendering him to their bond.

Red fell against Sebastian, releasing his dick from his mouth. He used his tongue — unnaturally long for a human — to make sure nothing was left behind, enjoying every drop.

His breaths slowed, the need that made his heart seem to catapult from his chest finally easing to a bearable state. The power that had erupted the moment Sebastian touched him stuttered to a hum. He rocked against Sebastian, settling into the V of his thighs, laying his head on Sebastian's chest.

His lover's hands eased into his hair, pulling at the strands, lifting his head.

Sebastian's burning eyes stared at him. "What are you?"

Did Sebastian know what he was asking? Did he suspect something?

Red could try to play the moment off, but Sebastian still glowed, and Red was confident his own eyes would be twin shimmering pools of gold and could not be mistaken for human. It would be the first thing his mate would see. The test of light, able to see within and determine worthiness. If Sebastian was not found worthy, his soul would erupt from within, his body becoming an ashen husk.

But instead, Sebastian leaned back, totally depleted, naked from his waist down, his hands gently running over Red's head, waiting with a befuddled expression.

"I'm your mate, Sebastian." Red looked at him and waited.

Sebastian nodded, and a half-smile tugged at his lips. "Now, that's new." His head fell back, his hand falling away from the gentle massage of Red's scalp. "Your mate."

Sebastian's body shook, and Red leaned forward to better

see his face. Instead of fear as he'd expected, Sebastian was laughing.

"The most intense orgasm I've probably ever had, and then you say that, like something out a romance novel. And the way your eyes shine like a pair of headlights? Could just about believe it." He groaned. "Way to kill the tension. I'm hungry."

Red was, too, but not for the food that sat on the coffee table. He'd hoped Sebastian would surely see what was happening and know they weren't finished. But if Sebastian was hungry, he would fortify his patience and wait. His mate's nourishment was vital, his health priority. Red would see to that first, then fuck him blind.

Besides, Sebastian already stirred beneath him, as if he possessed the strength to get Red off him. Or do anything other than submit.

Red nearly growled, eager to stake his claim. But instead, he rose, calming his beast. Sebastian pulled up his pants, tucked himself back in, and walked to the kitchen. He held two gold plates and a few turquoise bowls when he returned. His mate obviously liked things bright, even his dinnerware.

"So, let's see what we have here, *mate*." Sebastian chuckled as he looked through the most oversized bag. "Oh my, did you buy the entire menu? This is amazing!"

Pride rose in Red's chest from the happy sounds Sebastian made as he went through the bags like a kid on Christmas morning.

He slid his tongue along his lips to capture more traces of Sebastian, then said, "Maybe not the whole menu, but I did get a few of the things we tried the night we went out. You know, on our first date."

Sebastian was in the process of spooning food on his plate when what Red said must have hit him. He nearly dropped the spoon and faced him, his gaze looking for something.

"Red," Sebastian enunciated slow and calm.

"Sebastian," Red returned with just as much calm.

"This is all a little strange. I mean, we meet. We go out. You come here and swallow my dick whole. Then you're making like we're a couple or something. I don't know. First, you should know that I don't do that couples thing, mate, or otherwise." Sebastian tried to make his point, his tone kind as he explained. "Besides, are you even gay?"

Red smiled, answering without hesitation. "No."

Sebastian looked skyward and shook his head. "Oh, this is too much." He returned to selecting pieces of chicken from the box.

Red realized he was hungry himself and could eat a plate or two. Then they would move this further.

"Okay, so this"—Sebastian waved a spoon between them—"whatever it is will not work. Friends. That would be good for us. Let's work on that." Apparently satisfied with what he'd said, he nodded while looking for whatever else he wanted to add to his plate.

"Friends? We're going to fuck, Sebastian. I'm going to sink my thick cock into your round ass and see how tight those muscles of yours can squeeze as you ride me. Gonna be so much more than your *friend*, Sebastian. But whatever keeps you happy for now. I'll give you a little time to get used to the idea." Red leaned over him, making sure his chest pressed against him and enjoying the shiver he felt as he pointed to the box on the left. "Now, I was told you would love these."

Red rummaged through the bag, feeling Sebastian's gaze on him, but he ignored him. He'd let what he said marinate. Then he was going to make his next move. He needed to help his mate get used to him, help him realize that he was in for the long haul, gay or not. If gay meant he could keep Sebastian, gay he would be. A word didn't matter. Having Sebastian forever did.

Oh, Sebastian was so full he had to lean back against the couch to stretch his stomach. And Red? Red was so crazy. How in the hell had he missed that? But then he'd only known the man for a day or two. Sometimes it took a while for crazy to appear. But whatever Red's mental state, it didn't exactly stop Sebastian from wanting what the man proposed.

Sebastian loved a nice hard dick in his ass, and he was sure what Red was packing would more than satisfy his needs. But clearly, Red had some other plans. Plans that used the word mate, speaking of forever. Forever love didn't last. Forever love disappeared when things didn't pan out the way a person expected. Forever love had an expiration date. He didn't want a forever love. But a right now fuck? He could handle that.

"What are you thinking about?" Red asked as he took the plate from Sebastian's hand and placed it on the antique chest that served as a coffee table.

Sebastian looked at Red, letting his gaze rove over Red's broad shoulders, his biceps, and the rock-hard abs he wanted to play like a violin with his tongue as the bow. Oh, yeah. And that dick. Red was packing, and Sebastian's mouth watered to see what that would feel like on his tongue, stretching his mouth as he tried to get it all in.

"I'm thinking a lot of things."

Red's gaze roamed over Sebastian's frame, a slow smile crossing his lips, a bit of mischief in those dark eyes. "Still just want to be my friend?"

Sebastian groaned. "Oh, this is crazy." He stood. Distance and space. If he could just get away from how amazing Red smelled, from the way heat seemed to roll off him and physically batter Sebastian's walls, he could think. This close, all he could think of was stripping himself and falling on his belly, ass up for the man.

He felt Red behind him as he walked to the window, looking out into the night.

"You like bowling?"

That wasn't what he'd expected at all. "Bowling?"

"Yeah, bowling. Let's go bowling, play a few games, have a beer."

Sebastian turned, and Red was right there, his gaze boring into Sebastian's own. Red opened his arms, and before Sebastian could stop himself, he moved into them, enjoying the way they wrapped around him. Red felt good, right, making Sebastian feel safe, protected like Red was made just for him. He sighed.

"Fine." He was such an idiot.

"But, Sebastian?"

Sebastian nodded in response, inhaling the earthy scent that rose from Red, clinging to his skin, and made Sebastian want to live there.

"We're going to be more than friends. I'm going to own you."

Sebastian sighed as Red's hands reached beneath his ass and gasped when the man lifted him from the floor. Sebastian was helpless, and Red was strong, magnificently so. It did things to Sebastian to have someone who could move him like it was nothing, manhandle him whenever he wanted.

He wasn't a tiny thing. He had to be powerful to do his work, lifting, pulling, and turning people three times his size. But he also knew that he loved having someone else take charge of him. And it appeared Red wanted to do just that.

"Bedroom," Red growled.

"Oh." Had that squeak come from him? He had no idea he could even make that sort of noise.

"Yeah, I want to be inside you. We're making that happen right now. Bowling after."

CHAPTER NINE

R ed carried Sebastian into a room at the back as directed. He liked Sebastian's home, the colors, the way everything had a place. He could envision Sebastian taking care of the house he would provide for them, making it a sanctuary. Only days ago, he was telling himself he didn't want a mate, didn't need anyone. Now he was looking around Sebastian's apartment, deciding how Sebastian would fit in his life.

What would I need to adjust to make Sebastian mine?

Sebastian's bed was a king, perfect for them both. He tossed Sebastian on it, and his mate's heated look as he pulled off his shirt made his dick rock hard. Sebastian was gorgeous against the pillows that covered the bed, the gauzy bed covering a pleasing contrast.

"Like what you see?" Red flexed his pecs, displaying his chest for Sebastian's approval a second time.

There was that look again. The first time Red had removed his shirt in front of Sebastian, his mate had been quiet as a mouse. Now, Sebastian groaned, lip caught between his teeth as his gaze dragged over Red's nipples, slowly traveling down to his waist as if he was cataloging inventory.

But Sebastian didn't answer his question. Instead, he said, "Have you ever fucked a man before?"

Red paused, then smiled slowly, certain his grin was pure predator from the way his mate shivered. "No, Sebastian. I've never fucked a man before. Only women. But I'm going to fuck you. Make no mistake. You tell me what we need. I'll make it good, better than." He bent to remove his shoes, then unbuckled his pants. When he had everything off, his body completely naked, he looked up to see Sebastian staring. "Well, what do we need?"

"Lube. We need lube and condoms." When Sebastian glanced at Red's package, he added, "Oh, my ever-loving . . . Lube. Lots of lube."

Red laughed, gripping his length, enjoying how Sebastian's eyes widened. "Okay. You have that?"

Sebastian shook himself, his gaze still riveted below Red's waist. "Yes, of course, I do." He reached over and opened the nightstand drawer.

Red cocked his head to the side, unsure about the toys he saw there, but maybe they could play with them sometime. A brief thought of the other men Sebastian had been with crossed his mind, but Red wasn't going to worry about that right now. Sebastian was through fucking other guys. He was going to be entirely Red's after this. Red just needed to get Sebastian used to the idea. They'd get to know each other right after he claimed Sebastian's ass as his own.

"Get them," Red rumbled.

Sebastian quickly reached into the nightstand, pulling the items from the drawer. When he had them both, he turned back to Red.

"Now, if you want those clothes, you need to take them off. If I do, I can promise you won't be able to wear them again."

Oh, God. Sebastian was beyond wanting, because Red was hitting all his buttons. Hell, he'd fallen right into desperation. Red stood at the end of his bed, the glow of the light around him casting shadows in the room, like a warrior ready to conquer, and Sebastian was the spoils from the battle.

His eyes were intense, burning Sebastian from where he

stood. That wicked glow was there again, and Sebastian realized it wasn't his imagination. He'd thought earlier that there was something odd there but had chalked it up to the light in the room. Now, he wasn't so sure.

"Now," Red ordered.

Sebastian immediately felt precum leak from his hard as granite dick, along with his hole clenching, so eager to enjoy that massive dick standing between Red's tree trunk thighs like a third arm. He needed it inside him, drilling him. Fuck, it was going to hurt going in, and Sebastian would love every second. Some burn with his pleasure? That was for him.

He pulled off his clothes quickly because he did love the powder blue sweater he wore and his skinny jeans. They'd cost him a pretty penny, and the way Red was looking at him, he'd keep that promise of ripping them apart. When he was completely naked, Red seemed to grow in stature, longer, thicker than before. Sebastian glanced behind Red and almost swallowed his tongue.

The shadows on the wall did not reflect the man that stood above him. Sebastian glanced at Red quickly, then back to the wall where he saw wings, wings spread wide and open, and a head larger than Red's own. Maybe he'd had more to drink than he thought, if his vision created images that made no sense whatsoever.

"Shit, Red, the light's playing some serious tricks over there. Your shadow looks like it belongs to an animal. Am I that drunk? I can't be." One barely finished beer did not make him drunk. And yes, he was tired, but he wasn't that exhausted. If anything, he was a bundle of nervous energy anticipating more of what Red had to offer.

Red smiled, his grin wide and filled with teeth. "Get yourself ready, Sebastian. I want inside you."

Red groaned as he ran his hand from root to tip, drawing his thumb over the head of that giant monster between his legs. Then he stuck his thumb in his mouth, licking the shiny wetness. Sebastian was jealous as hell. He wanted to taste that himself, see if everything about Red was as good as it looked.

"I want that," Sebastian groaned.

"I'm ready to give it to you, baby." The heat in Red's eyes was enough to singe Sebastian's flesh. "Now, quick wasting time and get your hole ready."

Sebastian dropped the condom and quickly opened the bottle of lube in his hand. Squeezing a puddle of the stuff out, he parted his legs and stuffed himself with his fingers, making sure he was good and ready. He moaned, stretching himself, pushing deep because Red was going to make a profound impression when he fucked him.

Sebastian looked at Red while he prepared himself, moaning from his own touch. Red's gaze tracked his movements as he trailed his hand faster over that big red dick of his. When Sebastian wrapped his hand around his own dick, searching for his pleasure, he was immediately interrupted.

"Stop," Red ordered, one hand pulling at Sebastian's ankle until he'd dragged him to the bed's edge. "All the way. Wider. Hold your knees."

Sebastian did as told, trembling as he waited.

He loved the way Red looked at him. He knew his legs were long, and the way Red's eyes fell on his hole only made him more eager to be fucked.

Had Red ever been with a man? Did he know how he made Sebastian feel?

Sebastian just wanted the man inside him, making himself at home.

Red leaned over Sebastian, dick in hand, and pushed the crown against Sebastian's entrance. The size of his dick stretched longer, and Sebastian's eagerness grew with his anticipation.

CHAPTER TEN

R ed readied himself to bond with his mate. He looked up at Sebastian, loving the way those brown eyes took him in. He thrust inside, and Sebastian gasped, then moaned in pleasure. Red kept going, kept pressing until his length had found its way home completely inside Sebastian's body.

"Oh, God. Fuck, so fucking huge. Damn, you fucker. God, Red."

Red laughed into Sebastian's neck, loving the sounds, the grunts Sebastian made each time he thrust. Sebastian's long legs coiled around his waist, hands stuttering over his heated skin as he buried himself as deep as he could go.

"Sweet. So sweet. Never knew this could be so good. Never knew being with you could be so good." Red reached beneath Sebastian, lifting him higher, gripping his ass so hard he knew his fingerprints would be left behind. That was perfectly fine with him. Any fool that took his life in his hands to see his mate's ass with his claiming marks all over him wouldn't live to see the next day anyway. Red smiled when Sebastian's groans became chants, his name on those delicious lips like a mantra.

"Yes, Sebastian. Yes, love."

Sebastian's eyes opened, shining brilliantly, his gasps echoing in the room. "More, fuck. More."

And Red gave him just that, pumping inside him again, pulling Sebastian tight against him. Their dance together was fiery and wild, their sounds of pleasure loud.

"I can't breathe. I need . . . More."

"I'll give you everything, Sebastian, all of me." Red pushed Sebastian's legs open wider, rocking inside. "You're so tight, Sebastian. I can feel your muscles squeezing me, baby." He groaned. "Fuck. I needed this, needed you. Thank you, Sebastian."

Sebastian smiled against Red's skin, licked him, and laughed when Red gasped.

"Oh, Red. You're welcome." Sebastian reached back, his hands on the headboard, pushing himself down over Red's length.

Red couldn't stop his growl when Sebastian shifted position. It was low subtle rumble, but it was enough to cause a hitch in Sebastian's movements.

"Red? Oh, fuck."

Red moved faster, like a freight train ramming himself into Sebastian's tunnel, his dick hitting Sebastian's spot with each thrust. His growling didn't stop, and Sebastian apparently wasn't blind to the fact that Red was growing, Red's grip tightening around him.

"Red?" Sebastian needed to say something, ask him what was going on, but Red buried himself between his legs, and Sebastian wasn't interested enough in conversation with how amazing he felt.

Sebastian stretched his neck back, loving the way Red held him, slamming inside, his body a bow, and Red the violinist. "So good. Baby, please. Oh. So good."

Red stopped moving, his lips locked over Sebastian's nipple as sharp teeth began to nibble. Red moaned as he started suckling, the vibrations thrumming through Sebastian nearly making him come right then. Sebastian looked down to see Red's gaze tracking him and trailing down the column of his throat, a question in the depths.

"What, Red? What is it?"

Red said nothing at first. Just tasted and touched as his dick slowly eased in and out of Sebastian's hole, stretching him greater than he'd ever been before, the sound of their joining wrecking him.

"You're so beautiful, Sebastian. I don't want this to end." The look Red held was one of longing. "Tell me you want this."

Sebastian moaned, his body humming as Red kept moving, his lips trailing to his other nipple, licking before he took the flesh between his teeth and bit down. It was sharp and delicious all at once.

"Red. Shit." Sebastian groaned, twisting and turning but unable to move as Red held him captive.

Red lifted his head. "Tell me you feel this between us."

"Red, I can't . . . I just . . . You can't ask me this right now, right here. It isn't fair." Sebastian whimpered as Red slid his hand around his cock, his thumb tracing over the slippery tip.

Red laughed. "Nothing's fair in love and war. Haven't you heard that?"

Red pulled out, wrapping his arm around Sebastian's waist and flipping him over.

Sebastian thrilled at the possessive way Red handled him, driving inside him again, his heavy balls slapping against Sebastian's heated ass. He encased Sebastian's dick with his fingers again. Then used his other hand to pull him impossibly close, so close they could practically be one body. The two of them began moving in sync, Sebastian groaning as Red took him, body and soul.

It could have been seconds later, but it felt like days, years when Sebastian finally came. His orgasm was so intense it was like being jettisoned from his body. Moments behind him, Red poured his seed into the condom, but he didn't stop. Red continued moving, pushing, and squeezing Sebastian tighter, whispering his name into his skin, across his neck. Red licked and nibbled, tasting him everywhere until his bites grew sharper, more profound.

Red's wet tongue lapped at his skin, satisfied moans following. Sebastian wasn't sure he could come again, but he was already getting harder.

"Red?"

Red pulled him closer, his body covering Sebastian completely, his dick still rigid, still pulsing within him.

"Red? What's going on?"

Red used one knee to spread him further, then locked one arm, immobilizing Sebastian.

"So sweet. So good. I never knew how good it could be to have this, to have you." Red's voice was harsher, rougher.

Sebastian moaned as Red moved faster, purposefully. Red's palm slid up Sebastian's belly, over his chest until his throat lay vulnerable in his grasp.

"Red?"

Red's fingers pressed deeper against the column of Sebastian's throat.

"I thought I could wait. Could let you decide, but I was wrong. I had no idea that fucking you, being inside of you, could do this to me, could make me need to claim you. That you would taste so good to me. Had no idea I was starving without you. Forgive me, Sebastian. Say you forgive me." Red was fucking him in earnest now, his movements more intense.

But it wasn't enough. Something was missing.

"Oh, Red. Red. I forgive you. I promise. I fucking forgive you." Sebastian's cheeks were wet, his tears falling on the pillow. He had no idea what Red needed from him. He didn't care. He just needed him to keep going. Shit, and he needed something else. "The condom, Red. Take off the condom. I need you to come in me. Please, Red."

This person begging for more couldn't be him. Sebastian knew what bodily fluids were good for. Trouble. He couldn't explain it, but when Red pulled out only to slam back in again, it was all he'd ever wanted.

"Yes, Sebastian. You feel it. I knew you did. Feel me, baby. Feel us."

Sebastian groaned, rocking his head back and forth against the sheets hot from their bodies. Red gripped him again, his mouth sliding over his shoulder.

"Tell me it's okay. Say it. Say yes to me." Red rode him harder then, his sounds animal-like this time, his fingers sharp, like they were claws instead of the smooth digits caressing his skin all over earlier. His dick was stretching Sebastian wider now, completely opening him up, and Sebastian couldn't move, could only accept as Red possessed him.

Sebastian was so close to coming again. He needed Red to go harder, faster. "Yes, Red. Yes, whatever you want, baby. Just keep going. I promise it's okay. I promise."

Then Sebastian screamed, the sound bottoming out as the pain sliced at him, ripping through every cell of his body when Red clamped his mouth over the vein in his jugular, but Red didn't let go. He fucked him deep, hard, and long, still drinking Sebastian in. His swallows were vigorous against Sebastian's skin. Sebastian had no control over his body as another orgasm overwhelmed him. A tsunami of feeling rushed through him as he was held captive by Red, who only continued to drink. When Sebastian's eyes closed, he felt gentle licks along his skin and savored Red's whispered words.

"Thank you, Sebastian. Rest now, love. Rest."

Sebastian immediately fell into darkness.

CHAPTER ELEVEN

R ed stared at his sleeping mate. Sebastian was beautiful, the lines of his body sleek and powerful. He was slim, but he wasn't skinny. Red could tell Sebastian worked hard as he drew his finger along the sinewy muscle of his back. He traced the dragon tattoo as it curved around Sebastian's side, across his ribs, the tail of the creature settling at the curve of his thigh. It was a nice piece, an honor to a race that should have died out centuries ago. Red wondered about the choice of a dragon. What was it about them that fascinated Sebastian enough to have it cover his skin in brilliant shades of cerulean and emerald, fiery reds that blazed? It was magnificent, so beautifully rendered it seemed like it could fly away from Sebastian's body and place humanity at its feet rather than hide within the shadows.

Hide, like Red's people were forced to, because time hadn't stopped. It continued with its technology and change, causing a race that had thrived for thousands of years to remove itself from the awareness of man.

"Hello, brother," Red whispered, tracing the dragon's claws. "I miss flying with you."

Sebastian stirred, but rather than waking, he stretched and bent until his body settled into the curve of Red's embrace, seeking his closeness.

Red smiled. Sebastian might not have accepted him, laughing when Red told him he was his mate, but his body knew where he belonged and who he belonged to. He placed his hand on Sebastian's hip, squeezing gently. Red leaned over and drew his tongue along the puckered flesh where he'd tasted his mate's blood. "Mine," he whispered, and his dick hardened at the thought of retaking Sebastian.

Sebastian moaned, the sound both erotic and enticing.

Red slid his hand down Sebastian's hip, pulled his leg up, and pushed his dick between Sebastian's thighs. The noise that followed was pure need. Red groaned as he opened his mouth over his mark, taking the flesh between his lengthening canines, anticipating his mate's taste.

"Red. Please." Sebastian begged when Red took one of his nipples between his thumb and index finger, pulling and rolling the flesh until it pebbled. Sebastian reached back, grasping Red's body, hips rocking against his cock. "Please."

Red was helpless against a request for what he would die to have again.

"Get it."

Sebastian reached up, and Red almost whimpered with how close his dick's head was to Sebastian's rim. Sebastian thrust the bottle into Red's palm. It didn't take long, seconds before his dick was covered in the slick and shoved so far up Sebastian's ass, he could live there, safe and settled within his mate's body.

He thrust deep and long and hard. He rode Sebastian, who screamed and cried and begged for more, begged him with his body and his words to never to leave, just to keep going, to fuck him forever.

Red promised then and there that he would. It was a promise he would keep.

Later, Red sat in a chair, a beer in his hand, some fancy brew that came from nowhere near the distilleries he typically visited. He held the delicate bottle up and squinted at the label, wondering.

The warmth that surrounded him from being in his mate's place was a feeling he had no desire to lose. It felt like home.

For too long, he'd drifted from one woman to another, from one body to another. Not anymore. No. His heart would be with his mate and all body parts associated from now on.

Red looked back at the little bottle. It wasn't bad. Wasn't great, either, but it wasn't bad. He sighed and placed the bottle on a ceramic turquoise and coral coaster. It was a pretty thing, like everything in Sebastian's home. He looked around and noticed the paintings on the walls, the plush furniture, the rug with the weave long enough to bury his toes in for the first time. It was nice, comfortable, and suited his mate. He again imagined the place Sebastian would make for them, the home he would create. He was more than ready for that.

He wasn't surprised when his phone rang with the tone he used for Jacobi. The drumbeats suited the wanna-be musician, who was still unsure of his footing. Jacobi's destiny was more than working his father's lands, but he was still afraid of stepping out. The only thing Red could do was to be there for him when he finally made the decision. Settling back against the comfortable seating, he picked up the phone and answered.

"'Lo, Jacobi."

"So, how did it go?"

"How did what go?" Red laughed when Jacobi huffed in frustration. "It went fine, Jacobi. My mate is resting in bed now."

"And you're where?"

Red could hear it in Jacobi's tone, the wonder of why he would be anywhere else but where his mate was. "Sitting here talking to you. I knew you'd call. You wouldn't be able to help yourself, but if it comforts you, I told Sebastian I was his mate."

There was a long pause.

"Sebastian. Never heard of a woman being called Sebastian," Jacob said.

"Well, it's because it ain't a woman." Red waited and was not disappointed.

Jacobi laughed. "A man. Wait until they hear that. Me, I'm pan. But you? Straight as an arrow, or you were?"

"Still straight. If I'm to be labeled anything, it's that I'm Sebastian."

"Well, then."

Red listened until Jacobi got himself together and the chuckles dissipated, then he asked, "You okay?"

"Yes. Just needed a moment. So you told your male mate that he was actually your mate? What did he say?" Jacobi's words were slow and careful this time.

"He laughed."

"Laughed?"

"Yeah, but when I claimed him—"

"Wait, you did what?" Shock this time.

"You heard me, little brother."

"No, I didn't because it sounds like you claimed your mate without him fully understanding what a claim would do to him, to his life. If he laughed . . ." Jacobi was the younger of the two of them, but all their lives, he'd been the more serious, the one who dictated what needed to be done on the farm in his father's place and handled the encroaching of their people near their land. He was a leader, born to it.

"Oh, he did. Basically told me how silly I was right after the best orgasm he'd ever had."

"Well, there's that, but seriously, Red," Jacobi pleaded.

"Yes, I know, Jacobi. When we went for round two, I couldn't help it. In my defense, I told him. He knew. When I asked for permission, he said yes. In fact, he begged me."

"Red . . ."

"Enough, Jacobi. I hear him moving now. I need to be with him."

"When he sees the mark, Red—"

"Fuck! Jacobi, it will be fine."

"Who are you trying to convince? Me or you?"

Red hated to admit it, but Jacobi was right. He was trying to convince himself. What had he been thinking? "I'll talk to you later, okay?"

"Yeah, okay. And watch your back. Dad's still on high alert here."

Red didn't like the sound in his brother's voice. Sounded like his father wasn't the only one worried.

"And you? What do you think?"

"Yeah, I'm thinking he has reasons to worry, Red. When I checked the perimeter yesterday, something was off. Mom's wards were in place, but something or someone had been messing with them, digging. I think they're trying to find a vulnerability point. And Red, that vulnerability could be anywhere. It could even be someone. This thing with your man is new. Being with a man is new. Don't be stupid. Keep your eyes open." Jacobi sighed. "Look, I have to go. Have to get up early in the morning."

"Going flying?"

"No, but my wings are itching to. Give me a call later. Oh, and if you could record when your mate sees—"

"Oh, fuck you, Jacobi!" Red clicked off. He reclined, drink in hand, but put it down when he just didn't have the interest anymore. Listening, he heard Sebastian get out of bed, a bed he was looking forward to climbing back in again. He stood, but the sound of the bathroom door opening and closing reached him. He waited.

He didn't have to wait long.

"What the ever-loving fuck is this? Red!"

Red got his ass moving before his shrieking his mate woke up the entire building and some good Samaritan called the police.

CHAPTER TWELVE

Sebastian wasn't going to hyperventilate, no matter what was on his skin, because there was no way what he was seeing was real, right? He was dreaming. Yes, that was what it was. He closed his eyes.

Okay, Bastie.

Yes, he was using his childhood nickname. He'd never tell his mom he called himself the name when he was stressed. And right now, stressed didn't even cover it. Right now, a stampede of voracious butterflies was battling in his chest. There would be carnage and bloodshed.

He took a deep breath.

When I open my eyes, there won't be a huge tattoo covering my upper torso, swirling around my nipples with some type of scrolled writing ending below my neckline. It's all part of a dream, and I'll wake up.

He opened his eyes, and then he screamed. Again.

Arms surrounded him from behind, strong and warm, a broad chest blanketing his back. Red. Red's head was on his shoulder in the mirror's reflection, a soft smile on his face.

"It's beautiful, Sebastian. I had no idea what it would look like on you. I've only seen pieces of my mother's, but if hers is anything like yours, it has to be something. It compliments your dragon."

Sebastian opened and closed his mouth like a fish trying to grasp air. He could hear his jaw pop with the movement. Red traced the skin covered in ink, the tips of his fingers making Sebastian shiver.

"This is my claim, my mark. You wear my crest, a sign to my people that you belong to me." Red turned him gently, sliding his hands over the tattoo, bending to taste and nip as he did so. "So beautiful." Reaching down, he took Sebastian's dick in hand and tugged. "All of you." Then, he knelt.

Sebastian should have stopped him, but the sight of his fantasy on his knees in front of him was a dream realized. And having the heat from Red's mouth envelop his cock nearly made Sebastian's knees buckle. He moaned when Red used that fascinating tongue of his to lap at his dick, drawing a line from his balls to the tip and swallowing him in again.

"Red, I need to know . . ." But he couldn't complete the thought. He was too busy enjoying the way Red worshipped his body. The way Red's hands held his legs, rocking him in and out of his mouth, encouraging him to fuck his face. "Red? Oh, you sexy bastard you, this is so unfair."

At Red's muffled chuckle, Sebastian gasped, because hell if that didn't just almost make him come right there. He shoved his dick in harder, feeling the head of his dick go deeper into Red's squeezing throat that just felt too perfect for words. Fuck words right now. He pumped himself back and forth, grabbing Red's head to help him move just the way he needed.

Then, before he knew it, a tingling teased his balls, and he erupted, groaning as he emptied himself down Red's throat. He opened his eyes, because he'd apparently closed them when Red was using that magic tongue of his to blow his mind and his dick.

Gazing up at him was the beautiful man himself, that ginger hair wild with the way Sebastian's fingers had torn through it. Red's eyes, though, those hazel eyes stared at him, the crooked smile worming its way into his heart. A heart that beat so fast it could easily be the entire percussion section of an orchestra. The heart protected by muscle, bone, and flesh.

The flesh decorated with new ink or something. And that right there was enough to make him fall back against his sink.

"What have you done to me?" Sebastian shouted, his throat wrecked from the cry that ripped out of his throat when his body betrayed him.

Red leaned back, but even on his knees — having just swallowed Sebastian's seed and still licking his lips — Sebastian felt the power that radiated from the man. An energy that hadn't dimmed since the first time he sat beside Red in gun class.

"I told you, baby. You're my mate."

Sebastian tried to move back when Red stood. Had that been him, he would have toppled over, but Red rose easily, fluidly with a grace that made Sebastian itch to touch the man.

Sebastian shook his head. "Mate?"

"Yes. I'm sorry it took me so long to figure it out. I never thought I'd have one, and I certainly never thought it would be a man."

"Oh," Sebastian said. "You're not — "

"Gay," Red supplied, bending down to kiss Sebastian gently, feeding him a tongue flavored with Eau de Sebastian.

The thought of tasting himself on someone else would normally make him squeamish, but he welcomed it from Red. Nevertheless, the ease of his acceptance unnerved him. He shook his head, trying to regain the balance he needed to have this conversation. However, the sight of Red's fucking nipples was distracting him.

"Clothes. Clothes are a necessity right now." Yes, that was it. Put something on the man, and Sebastian wouldn't feel like taking one of those buds in his mouth or the need to grab that enormous dick tormenting him with its semi-hardness. He shivered. "Yes. Clothes."

Sebastian eased around a smiling Red, the heat in his eyes shorting out his brain. No, he would not turn and face the wall and beg the man to shove his monster dick up his ass. Instead, he kept said ass moving.

Moments later, Red finally wore a shirt that stretched across his juicy pecs. Sebastian realized that clothed or not, the man was still a distraction, perhaps even more so with the hint of flesh peeking out in those dinosaur-covered briefs he wore.

"Dinosaurs?"

Red smiled bashfully and shrugged. "I like them."

"Okay." Sebastian nodded slowly, not bothering to comment on how fucking cute that was.

Red sat on the couch, his muscular thighs relaxed, an arm casually thrown on the back of the seat. Sebastian was standing, trying his damnedest not to crawl his way between the man's legs. He was rational. Hell, he was a nurse. He saw crazy all the time. Earlier, when Red said he was his mate, Sebastian had laughed. Now, when he looked like he'd taken an involuntary trip to a tattoo shop, he couldn't figure out where his judgment had failed him. Had Red drawn this shit all over his body? He looked down. No, there was no way. He looked back at Red, who sat and waited too patiently, too calmly, and it was starting to piss him off a little.

"So . . . mate?"

Red nodded, then drew a hand along his thigh, those long fingers touching skin Sebastian wanted to worship.

"Stop that."

"Stop what?"

"You know the fuck what."

Red lifted a brow. "Sebastian, baby. Why don't you come sit down?"

"Oh, you'd like that, wouldn't you? For me to come over there and throw myself over the couch so you can fuck my ass."

Red raised both brows at that. "Uhm, while I would be happy to have your ass again, that's not why I'm asking you to sit next to me. I just want you to be near me, close to me. You seem so far away."

Red smiled with a wide grin, boyish and cunning. He knew exactly how he affected Sebastian.

And even though Sebastian was trembling inside, his fear didn't stop him from wanting to climb Red like a tree. "What happens if I sit down?" Sebastian asked.

"Well, before I throw you over the couch and fuck said sweet ass, maybe we talk about the crest. We start with who I am and what you mean to me. Is that okay?"

Red reached out, and Sebastian longed to go to him, to place his hand in the palm of Red's much bigger one and trust. Trust was hard.

How many times have I trusted someone only to have my heart broken? Am I willing to risk myself all over again?

He'd already gone this far. *Reach out.* When his fingers touched Red's, his skin burned. He gasped, but the feeling wasn't enough to make him stop. He could have. He could have told Red to get out of his apartment, delete his number, and never see him again.

But that wasn't what he wanted to do. He wanted to bathe in Red's aura and savor his heat.

"There you go, sweetheart. Come on over here now." Red gently tugged him onto the couch.

Sebastian fell into Red's arms, and his new tattoo suddenly sent sparks over his chest and down his legs. Fire spun around his waist and kissed his shoulders, licking at his ears and rushing over his toes. He was surrounded by flames that tingled but surprisingly didn't burn.

Red looked at him with awe. "I always wondered what it felt like. My mom never really told me. I've seen bits of hers, but they only appear when the two of them are looking at each other funny. You know."

Sebastian burst out with giggles. "What, Red? Too shy to talk about your parents getting busy?"

He laughed harder when Red tickled him and moaned when the touches became more erotic, his mouth captured with a heated kiss.

He let his head fall against Red's neck and breathed him in. "It feels like tiny flames are dancing on my skin, like an allergic reaction, and I need to use an epinephrine injector before speeding to the ER."

"Oh," Red said. "I hadn't thought of that." He smiled before nibbling Sebastian's shoulder gently.

"Let me guess. You thought something romantic like you'd read in a book, and the character's all *Red, touch me again. Let these flames take us together!* Nope. Definitely, an allergic reaction to whatever funky venom your body's got going on."

"Huh," Red said. "So guess you don't want this." He lifted his head and stopped the lovely things he was doing to Sebastian's skin.

"Never said that. You asked me how it felt. Plus, I look like I got hit with a gang of tattoo artists who wanted to make sure every part of my body was marked *property of Red* and his weird as hell genetic wizardry. But fucking you? Oh, I want that so badly I'm willing to wear this full-body tramp stamp with pride after I understand what the fuck it is, and more importantly, who you are."

Red smiled. "I don't know what I expected, and that's what I like about you. You surprise me, Flirty."

Sebastian raised a brow, confused. "Flirty?"

"Yeah, it's how I thought of you the first day I met you. Kind of stuck with me." He kissed Sebastian on the nose.

Sebastian sighed, too enamored by the big doofus to worry about what might be his first pet name.

First?

Was he settling into the idea of a relationship with Red?

Red and Flirty? He laughed. It sounded like the title of a romance novel. But this was real life, and mates were things of fiction, weren't they?

"I'm listening, so start explaining."

Chapter Thirteen

R ed hesitated, staring at his mate. So maybe Jacobi was right, and he should have given further thought to how Sebastian would respond to a marking.

His mother wore her marks with love, often touching a darkened shadow here or there. The looks she would give their father were their secret messages communicated without a single word.

He had been lying to himself, saying a mate wasn't a dream of his. It was. And Sebastian drew him like a hummingbird to a morning bloom, if he was honest with himself. He wanted to sample him and keep coming back for more.

I'm not going to fuck this up.

Or he would try his damnedest not to.

He took a deep breath and dove in.

"So let me get this straight," Sebastian said while he paced the length of his living room. "You're a griffin."

"Yes. I've been—"

"Nope, nothing else for now. I'm processing and wrapping my head around information I never imagined I would hear." Sebastian cocked his head to the side. "Maybe in a movie or a book or something. I mean, I do have a thing for dragons, but they're not even real."

Remembering the skilled rendition of a dragon on his mate's body, Red said, "Yes, they are . . . or were. It's been years since I've seen one, flown with one. And though the one on your body is beautiful, I can't help but say I'm a little jealous."

"Wait. Are dragons real? What about unicorns? No." Sebastian held up a hand. "No, don't answer that. I'd rather get this worked out first. Unicorns can wait. Even dragons can wait. And I'd be lying if I didn't admit you being jealous doesn't make my dick hard a little."

The heated look Sebastian threw Red's way had him wanting to pull that long body against him again, showing him what jealousy made him want to do.

Red growled.

Sebastian's eyes widened. "Fuck. I think I like that."

Red moved to stand, but Sebastian shot his hands out. "No. Still processing."

For now, Red let him have his way. But he fully intended to have his way later. He sat back against the couch and ran his hand over his dick instead.

"No, none of that either. All I want to do is climb between your legs and suck your cock into my mouth when you do that. Now, stop it."

Sighing, Red took his hand off himself and rested it on the back of the couch. "Better?"

"Yes," Sebastian responded with a quick huff. "A griffin. So when I saw that shadow of your body, it was a griffin's silhouette. And what is a griffin anyway? Do you really have—"

"The head of an eagle, body of a lion, and wings? Yes. Though my wings are more leather than feathers. As a docent, I was born distinguished from others. Our entire line is."

"And that's the other thing. Docent? I mean, it's a professor, right?"

Red loved watching Sebastian trying to work through all he'd heard. His strides back and forth were distracting, his body begging Red to touch and tease.

He nodded. "While that's one definition, the other would be a guide, which is what we are known as. We are born to guide, while others are to protect. Our people are the defenders of good, the enemy of evil. Or at least we are supposed to be."

And that was his family's worry. It should have gone against the clan's blood for the current Ilios to want to take and use rather than share and give. It was in the genetics of a griffin to be just and fair, to conquer evil. Somehow, that had changed, and the poison leaching through the clan worked to destroy them all. They were people of the sun, keepers of knowledge and history. Over time, that knowledge had produced wealth that seemingly acted adversely for their clan.

Fortunately, his father had seen what could happen when they rejected his bond, human or not. Things had only become worse for others. The Ilios ruled with tainted claws, using and abusing any who would go against him. Instead of steady growth, they experienced a decline. While his family had separated themselves from the clan, others who sought sanctuary still found their way to the safety of their farm.

Red had always been curious about the others, but he wouldn't push his father's need to protect them. They kept their distance, or at least he had. Jacobi was different, and Red could feel his brother's need to help where he could.

"Supposed to be." Sebastian cocked his head. "Sounds like there's a story behind those words."

"There is, but there's no use sharing that right now. Come sit with me."

Sebastian shook his head. "Nope, not yet. The minute I let myself get close to that body of yours, I'll lose my head."

"Is that such a bad thing, baby?"

Sebastian blushed, and it was the prettiest thing Red had seen in a month of Sundays.

His mate looked up at the ceiling and then at Red again. "I

don't know why I even like that so much. I'm not into endearments. But you call me baby, and I want to melt. Is that the mate thing, the bond you mentioned?"

"I don't honestly know. I'd like to say it's just the way you feel about me, you know. I know it's fast and all. I mean, we barely know each other."

"None of what you're saying is making me feel better right now."

Red raised his hand, pleading, "Wait."

"I am."

"Thank you." Red smiled. "While we barely know each other, I feel like we were meant to be. I feel it in here." He touched his fingers to his heart. "And here." He touched an index finger to his temple. "I know you're mine. I just need you to know that, too."

Sebastian sighed. "I feel something, Red, but I'm not even sure what it is. When I didn't see you, I ached like something was missing, and when you're next to me, you're all I can think about. But is that enough?"

"It's a beginning."

"Yes, it is." Sebastian laughed gently. "So there's a bad guy?"

Red didn't want to tell Sebastian about that. He wanted more time to get to know him without bringing in a bogeyman.

"You might as well tell me everything, Red. I'm going to find out."

"Can I hold you while I tell you that? I'm afraid."

Sebastian looked into Red's eyes, searching. Whatever he found there made him rush forward and fall into Red's embrace. "You don't have to be afraid, Red. I have you."

Red kissed Sebastian's lips gently, breathing in his scent, savoring their closeness. He never wanted to let Sebastian go, and the fear that his following words would chase him away was palpable.

"I'm a docent. Part of that role is being a king detector for our people."

"Griffin people? You can be people?"

"Yes, Sebastian. We're people." Red kissed him on his nose. "But just like you have a hard time seeing griffins as people, we have those in our clan that see humans as less than. Barbaric. My father is a griffin, but my mother is a human witch, and their relationship was considered dicrac to our clan."

"Dicrac?"

"Yes. Forbidden. Griffin mates with griffin, and it's forbidden to do otherwise. We keep to ourselves. We aid humans, look out for them, assist with the knowledge we have collected over the centuries. We do not marry them and create little forbidden fruit."

"And that's what your father did."

"That's exactly what he did, but he's still a docent, which means the gift would follow in his line, tainted by a human witch or not. His progeny are still valuable, particularly the eldest son, as the gift is passed on to the firstborn child."

Sebastian settled into his arms, and Red's beast was just as pleased as its counterpart.

"And while we were not welcome as part of the clan, the gift and its appearance are all that matters. But the gift only appears when we meet our mate and the mate wears our crest."

He ran his fingers down the front of Sebastian's canary yellow hoodie and then slipped his fingers beneath the fabric. The marks were warm, kissing his fingers, whispering *mine,* proving Sebastian was his mate.

Sebastian moaned. "Just you touching my skin is driving me crazy. I want to bend over and beg you to fuck me." He groaned and pulled away. "But there's more to this story. I want to hear it all. I need to know what you're so afraid to tell me."

Red sighed, and while he didn't let go completely, he did settle back. "With you having my crest, they will want to re-claim my mate and me. With you being human, they may try to take us apart."

"Take us apart? Somehow I don't think it's just breaking us up, you mean."

Red was afraid of this, of Sebastian having to choose be-tween what they shared, which was new and fragile, or to protect himself from being a target just because he was hu-man.

"No, I don't. My father gained his birthright when he met my mother, but no matter the power of his gift, her humanity was the target of anger and hate. He chose her, and they left."

"And now it's your turn."

"It is," Red affirmed. "I can see now, feel the strands of our people. I can touch their bonds, especially the ones who've chosen to move near us. I'm tied to them more than I have ever been."

Sebastian slid his body closer. "What's that feel like?"

"It's tangible like I'm a part of them. So rooted. It's as if I'm a tree, and the people are leaves. I feel them branch out and can distinguish each one. Even now, I know there are those with babies . . . some new, some months along. I feel their pulse."

"That's insane." Rather than freaking out, Sebastian seemed intrigued.

That gave Red hope. "Yeah. Yeah, it is."

"And this happened the moment you claimed me."

"The very second you wore my mark, I knew who I was, who they were, and what was to come."

"And this knowledge is dangerous."

"Deadly for us all. They will want to take you, see if they

can control the gift. Use it for their own."

He told Sebastian about the Ilios wanting to keep his title and the power that went along with it.

"But if I'm the one who helped you discover yourself, know this ability, then why do they believe harming me will help? We're tied together. While this all still seems insane to me, it's even crazier for them to want to destroy the person who helped you gain this." Sebastian's expressive hands waved around for emphasis.

"Sadly, the Ilios doesn't understand this or refuses. Our people suffer because of him, and instead of growing, we're regressing."

"No, you're the ones who chose to leave, or your father did. So your family is playing with a full deck. That other guy and his minions? Not so much."

"Unfortunately, it's the ones like Laith who are determined to keep things in the past. Progress takes work. It takes a voice and knowing when some things are just plain wrong. Our people should have loved my mother for the protection she could offer and who she is as a person. Instead, she became a target. It's what I should have thought about before pursuing you, but I don't have any regrets." He kissed and enjoyed the curve of his mate's lips.

Sebastian's smile was soft, showing a bit of vulnerability. "Well, I still have questions, but I don't have any regrets, either."

"Baby, I'm here to answer any question you have. I want you to feel safe with me." He kissed Sebastian lightly, trying to keep things casual, but he couldn't help pulling Sebastian a little closer. "I don't want you to have regrets. You make me want to prove to you that we're worth it."

Sebastian leaned in and kissed him this time. Again, the kiss was tender and sweet, with a bit of heat when Sebastian nipped at his lip, sending a direct zing to his dick.

"I think we can be. I just want to know what we're in for."

Red nodded. "That's fair. I can't honestly say what they will do, but whatever it is, it won't be good." In another breath, he said, "I want you to meet my family."

"What?" Sebastian's voice raised an octave higher than it was before. "No."

Red sat up, reaching for Sebastian, who already stood across from him, arms wrapped around himself protectively.

"Sebastian?" Red called, holding his hands out. "What's wrong?"

"I want this. I want you. I do, even though it goes against all my defenses. But from what you've said so far, I don't believe your parents know there's the possibility of you being with a man." He pointed to himself. "This man. And I'm sorry, but I will not be the bitch that breaks up your family. I've already lost mine. I won't let you lose yours."

"Wait."

Red stood, but Sebastian had opened the bedroom door and slammed it behind him, leaving Red confused and wondering when everything had gone so wrong.

CHAPTER FOURTEEN

"So wait, Sebby, you had a big, strong, and thirsty man that wanted you, and you gave his ass up because you're worried about his family disowning him because of you?" Mavis's hair bounced along with the wine glass she gesticulated with, directing it toward Sebastian.

"Yes, I did."

"What is this fucked up thinking of yours? Shit, it's been how long now?" She burped.

Mavis was beautiful, and the woman lucky enough to snatch her up had to be ready for the contrast of supermodel looks with your favorite bro's behavior. Her black shoulder-length curls matched the zebra-colored nails on her fingers. She was a contradiction, and he loved every bit of her.

"Three weeks," Sebastian mumbled, and the answer hurt to say.

Mavis pointed one dagger-sharp nail in the air as if she were a lawyer preparing her case. "One, you barely get any as it is. Two, you fucking sigh every time you say his name. Three . . . shit . . . what's three? Oh . . . You are too damn awesome to become a crusty old cat man."

"Lady," Sebastian corrected.

"No, you're a man. I'm a lady." She let out another loud belch.

Cassandra giggled. "Yeah, lady."

"Oh, piss off, princess. I'm a lady. You let that hubby of yours know I could have made you a happy woman."

"If I was gay," Cassandra laughed.

"Yeah, well. If you were, there's still time to make better choices." Mavis snorted and leaned in for a kiss.

"Stop it. I think you've had enough to drink."

Before Cassandra could swipe the wine glass that was perilously close to spilling over, Mavis snatched it back and swigged.

"Shh. Now, we are here to talk about Sebby and his ridiculous choices."

"Sebby can make his own decisions."

"Yes, ones that will make him a cat man."

"Lady," Sebastian interjected.

"Whatever, heifer. Where's the pizza, and can we just turn this movie off? We're not even watching it. Aren't there enough Marvel movies by now?"

Sebastian and Cassandra crossed themselves.

"Sacrilege. Thou shalt not speak against the entertainment that is Marvel," Cassandra declared.

"Oh, fine. I dare either of you to tell me what's even happening. Sebby's been making moon eyes and sighing dramatically since we've been here and finished at least two bottles of wine. He's talked about this guy nonstop, and I think it's time he got his shit together and called the guy. We are ready to meet our future brother-in-law."

Sebastian sighed but quickly cut it off when Mavis rolled her eyes at him. "Fine. I miss him."

"Really. I'm baffled. I couldn't tell at all," Mavis slurred with loads of attitude.

"She does have a point, Sebastian. You like this guy. Why not just call?" Cassandra reasoned.

"And be the reason his family will have nothing to do with him? My father pretends like I don't exist, and my mother hardly speaks to me, too worried about what he'll say. She has to live with him. I don't. I've seen them during awkward holiday dinners, but I've made certain to be *at work* ever since the last horrible affair when no one talked to me."

"I'm sorry, baby, but that was her choice, and your stupid family who can't see what a jewel they have in you. Not everyone's like that. Our belching beauty over here is well-loved by her family." Cassandra pointed at Mavis while discreetly sliding the third wine bottle out of reach. "Right now, she's having her own little drama party of one and dragging us along with her. But we love her anyway, just like she and I love you, our beautifully misguided self-sacrificing boy."

Sebastian sighed, tears forming at the corners of his eyes. "I love you, too. This is just so hard for me, Cassy. I mean, I want him. Of course, I do, but what if it's his family he chooses instead of me? Where does that leave me?"

"What do you have to lose now, Sebby? I mean, really? If you don't give yourself a chance. Even if she." Mavis sighed.

"He," Sebastian corrected.

"He decides you're not woman enough." And then Mavis was crying again.

"Man," Cassy corrected.

"And dumps you for some silly little bitch she met at a potluck dinner at work. I hope she coughs up a furball."

Cassy gently removed the wine glass from their brokenhearted friend's grasp and set it aside, then tugged her into her arms and held her while she sobbed. Then, at Sebastian's raised brow, she smiled.

"And if I get dumped for some bitch at a potluck."

"We'll take care of you, too," Mavis sniffled.

Sebastian crawled to Mavis's other side and took a spot where he, too, could care for their girl.

A few hours passed, and Mavis was resting in a guest room, showered, and put to bed. Her gentle snores were interrupted by hiccups in her sleep, and Cassandra and Sebastian sipped at a glass of wine, enjoying another episode of their favorite show.

"Why do we watch this?" Cassandra asked. "None of them can cook."

"Because what they do accomplish is such a disaster, we can't wait to see the next one. I mean, they win an award for coming close even if it's disgusting and nowhere near the example. But, you know, they tried. That's the fun. They try, and everyone has a good time."

Cassandra nodded then turned to him.

He held up a hand. "Oh, I know that look. I'm not one of your children"

"No, you're not. You're one of my best friends who's a little afraid right now to try. And I get it." She angled her head toward the bedroom, where a restless Mavis sniffed in her sleep. "But sometimes you have to just go for it. It's fun, messy, and never what you expect it to be. It's hard work, but it can be a lot of fun. It's what you make it. But honey, you will never know if you don't try, and using his family as an excuse for you not being willing to fight for your happiness doesn't hold up."

"Fucking bitch," Mavis mumbled.

Sebastian and Cassandra turned to the room where Mavis still slept, talking in her sleep.

"And give Mavis some time. She'll be okay. She has us. We have each other." She turned back to the TV. "Oh, no. They're not going to eat that, are they?"

"They have to. Look, there she goes. Look at her face. Wait, there's our guy. Look at all those muscles." He sighed. "Red has muscles like that."

"Come here, silly. Let me hold you."

Sebastian put their wine glasses on the table and went into Cassandra's waiting arms.

"Give it a chance, sweetheart," she whispered.

Someone was knocking on Sebastian's door. If they didn't stop, they would wake up Mavis, and no one wanted that.

Cassandra's husband, Henry, had picked her up, bundling her off after she'd kissed Sebastian's cheek, leaving him to tidy up before going to his room to sleep. Henry was a good guy, quiet but strong. He was a good balance for Cassandra, who tended to light up a room. Sebastian would be lying if he said he didn't want something like that for himself.

Thankfully Sebastian didn't wake with a hangover because the knocking had not stopped.

"Sebastian, whoever the fuck that is, either let them in or tell them to go fucking home. If you don't, I will." Mavis was shouting but still sounded groggy.

"Don't worry, heifer. Sleep. I'm going now."

When he looked through the peephole, he didn't recognize the woman standing on the other side until she looked knowingly at the door and directly at him.

"Hi, there, Sebastian. I've brought you breakfast."

This woman was Red's mother. It was there in her hazel eyes and her knowing smile.

"Come on, love. Open the door. I would love to meet my son's mate. Perhaps have a peek at your mark."

Stunned, Sebastian opened the door and stood there gaping in shock.

"Oh, my. Perhaps you should cover that up, hm. While a beauty, it's not my eyes that should be seeing your appendage there."

Flushing, Sebastian turned, running to his room. Quickly, he dragged on a t-shirt and sweats while preparing himself to return.

Red's mother is in my home, and she brought food.

Mate, she called me his mate.

She knows about the mark.

Mavis is here.

With that final thought, he rushed back out to find Mavis

sitting at his breakfast counter, a muffin in hand, chatting with his . . .

What is Red to me?

His boyfriend, fuck buddy. Red was more than that. No, mate. Red was his mate, and though Sebastian struggled with what that meant, he knew any attempt to diminish what they were to each other wasn't fair to either of them.

He nearly choked when Mavis said, "So you're Red's mom, huh? This is so good. You know Sebastian's probably hiding in his room, right?"

"I am not," Sebastian defended even though he had considered the idea, waiting until she did whatever she had come to do and then leaving. But hiding in rooms had never been him. So he strode forward, head held high with butterflies moshing in the pit of his belly. "I'm right here."

Her golden gaze grasped him, warming him from the inside out.

"Ah, there you are, sweetie. You're just as beautiful as my son said you were." Red's mother wiped her hands on an apron Sebastian had never seen before and turned down the heat on the stove, where something delightful simmered in a sauté pan.

Then she did something Sebastian had longed for, had missed more than he realized.

She hugged him.

A mother's hug where his had been absent and sparing. He sighed, too afraid to let himself fall into the joy of being held and nurtured, the strength of the arms around him too beautiful to let go.

The tirade of tears came faster than he realized, his broken heart laid bare for all to see.

"Shhh, love. I'm here. We all are." And that was when Sebastian noticed the television was on, the sound of a game playing, and two prominent men watching with their shoes off and a drink in hand.

"When?" His hand gestured to the living room.

"Well, when my son said he'd met his mate, but that mate was afraid the family who would receive such a blessing would somehow reject him, we had to come. So now, come eat, and let's chat."

Sebastian glanced over at Mavis, who smiled back encouragingly. She looked exhausted, but her cheeks were rosy, and there was a glow that hadn't been there last night.

"Mavis, darling, could you get a few more plates from the cabinet?"

"Of course, Alice."

"Thank you—such a lovely girl. You be sure to visit the farm. We have nice neighbors with friendly daughters who are worthy of your time. I have one or two who I'd like you to meet when you're ready." She smiled at Mavis, who returned a watery grin.

Apparently, Sebastian hadn't been the only one needing some motherly care. Mavis's eyes were wet as she retrieved the desired plates and handed them to Red's mother, who kissed her on the cheek before pushing her toward the stool to sit again. "Oh, you finished your muffin. Now, a little juice, okay?"

Mavis nodded

Alice gave her a glass filled with orange juice that had not been in his refrigerator. She waited until Mavis sipped before calling, "Levi and Jacobi, come fix your plates." She turned to Sebastian. "Red's mate and I are going outside on that nice balcony of his to have a chat."

"Then I'll have my turn, wife," a powerful voice boomed from the living room.

"Yes, darling. It will be your turn to welcome our new son soon."

"Good. I'm being patient."

"Yes, my mate. You are." Alice clasped Sebastian's hand

and drew him to the balcony, pushing the door open and taking them out into the morning air.

"You know, it's nice here, not as nice as life will be on the farm for you, but I do see why you chose to stay."

He liked how his balcony overlooked a forest. It had been the view that had caught him. It was something about being near trees, his sanctuary from the city stress. Mornings, he would sit with a hot cup of coffee and prepare his mind for the day. Sometimes, he thought of him and Red enjoying that time together. But he'd left Red behind and stopped answering his calls.

"Yes, I like it."

"It's your affinity for nature, your gift for life that is a part of what makes you the choice mate for my son. My husband felt the stir of another and knew, but Red, bless him, is sometimes blind to what's right before him. But there you are." She pressed a warm hand against his cheek and caught his hand in her smaller one.

Sebastian smiled, unable to help himself. The warmth from this woman touched him. She was light, chasing the darkness away, removing the cobwebs from his heart.

"He told me."

"Good. He should have. I think my Jacobi had something to do with that. Jacobi likes things out in the open, no shadows, that one. He is such a leader, and though older, Red has always listened to him. So your mark should not have been a surprise to you, because Red should have prepared you."

"No, how many people would have been ready to hear about possibly being a mate? He didn't know."

"Even now, you defend him. You love my son."

"No, I've only just met him."

Her palm warmed against his skin, and Sebastian breathed her in, the scent of flowers touching his nose.

"A mother knows, and as your mother, I now know you.

What you have growing inside you is the bond of you and your mate, one that will only become stronger as you both learn to be honest with yourselves and with each other. And your fear of us casting away our son is without foundation. We need our son, and we need you."

"Red said—"

"That there are foolish people that tried to hurt me, a human. He told you about all my mate had to give up to have me in his life."

"Did he also tell you how I would have made that choice again, boy? That the love of my mate was worth having her and nothing else," a powerful voice interjected.

Red's father stepped onto the balcony, and though Sebastian's terrace was expansive, Red's father was not a small man. So Sebastian stepped back to give the man room.

"Levi," Alice scolded. "You were supposed to wait."

"I did, but I wanted to meet our new son and help you rid his mind of these anxious thoughts he carries."

The man was massive, as broad as Red or broader, and tall. His size was imposing, but Sebastian couldn't step back any further. So he stood his ground and waited to hear what Red's father had to say.

"Gentry tells me you're worried about us shunning our boy because his mate is a man. While I may worry how you'll bring forth young to continue the line, I don't care about what form you take. Our son's got it in his head you're for him. All that matters to me is that you be there to see it through. Neither his mother nor I have any right to choose who our boys love, man or woman." He looked around and took a deep breath. "I like it out here, Alice. Nice land back there."

"Yes, love. Good space."

"It is that. Be good for Gentry to share a flight with you out here so close to the forest. But with how wide your eyes are getting, I'm guessing you maybe didn't know our boy can fly."

"There are still things for me to learn." Flying wasn't going to be one of them. Sebastian only flew because it was necessary for work. He liked having his feet on the ground.

"Well, Gentry is ready to show you. That's why we're here, after all. We couldn't have found your place on our own. Of course, you have our boy to thank for that. Likes to cut to the chase, and he figured the best way to calm those fears of yours was to meet it head-on."

Levi placed his heavy hands onto Sebastian's shoulders.

"Sebastian, I will never do to our children what others did to me. Love looks beyond what's physical. It's about what beats in the heart, what gives us joy and hope, makes us want to be better. I would give my life for my Alice, human or not. She's my whole world, and she blessed me with two sons who make me proud every day."

"Aw, thanks, Dad. We're plenty proud of you, too," another voice responded from the doorway.

Suddenly there were two giant men on Sebastian's balcony.

Should I pray it doesn't crack and we all fall to our deaths?

"And now you, too, Jacobi? Look at his eyes, wide as saucers. I'm sorry, Sebastian, they were supposed to wait." Alice fixed her gaze on both her husband and her son, but neither looked apologetic.

"Yes, ma'am, we know, but I wanted to meet him. Dad was already out here, so . . ." He shrugged, and the shirt he was wearing barely contained the muscles underneath.

"Hi, Uhm, Jacobi," Sebastian spoke tentatively, certain the thread of fear underlying his words could be heard.

He reached out a hand to shake Jacobi's hand, only to have Jacobi pull him into a hard bear hug. His grunt was challenging to hide, and when Jacobi sniffed his neck and into his collar, he gasped in surprise.

"Clean," Jacobi announced, then pushed Sebastian over to

his mother. "Honest, too. He'll make a suitable mate for my brother. So you're a nurse, too? That's useful."

Confused and still trying to get over being sniffed as if he were a package and Jacobi a drug dog, he nodded. "Uhm, yes. I'm a nurse. Traveling nurse."

"Yes, Red did mention that. Will you miss it?" Alice asked.

"Miss it," Sebastian questioned.

"Yes, when you stop traveling and begin your life with Red."

"Woah." He pressed a hand to his temple to stall the headache he knew was coming.

"Oh, no. You've done it now." Mavis said from the doorway. "Sebastian, honey. I'd ask if you need some air, but you're already outside. Wine?"

"It's too early." Sebastian closed his eyes as the beginning of a panic attack caught him in a wave.

"Oh, yeah. I'm coming. Everyone, get off the balcony. Give Sebby some room."

Mavis's hands were gentle as they rubbed circles in his palms. The footsteps of his guests grew quiet as they went inside, and it was just the two of them.

"There you go, babe. Listen to me breathe. In and out."

Gradually, the waves ceased, Sebastian no longer held in the panic attack's grip.

Someone eased a cool glass of water into his hand and helped him drink, his throat dry from the heaving breaths he'd had to take.

"Now, let's sit for a moment, okay."

Sebastian fell into his patio chair and sighed. "Mavis, this is happening. I just met a family, the family of a guy I want in my future."

"Yes."

Mavis waited patiently as Sebastian got his thoughts together.

"And they accepted me. Not only that, but they're also trying to plan a future for us, too."

"Yes, is that what sent you off?"

"I think. Sometimes I don't know the cause. It just happens, and I'm lost." He couldn't always identify the source. It had started years ago but rarely showed its face these days. Still, it happened.

"Typically, there's a trigger involved. And for you, I think it's the idea of a true relationship, honey, one where you won't be rejected. One you're afraid of losing."

"Like you did?"

Mavis laughed. "Yeah, well. If I thought about it, she and I weren't going to make it. I need, no, I deserve someone who accepts me for me just like you do. I'm not refined or whatever she wanted, but I'm a good person with a fierce heart who will fight dirty for the person she loves if she has to. If someone can't appreciate that, spilt milk, you know?"

Sebastian sighed, easing the tightness around his chest from a lack of air. "Doesn't mean it doesn't hurt."

"Oh, baby, it does. Breaks my heart, but I'll get over it and her. Promise. Getting knocked down is not losing. Not getting up again is. Especially when there's someone in your corner to help."

Sebastian laughed softly and welcomed the hug.

Later, Sebastian sat at his kitchen table with Mavis and Red's family, eating breakfast and chatting. He was surprised at how comfortable he felt, and it made him happy. The tension that hung around his own family's events like a storm cloud didn't exist here. No, they chatted and enjoyed some stories about Red as a child. He could picture himself eager for times like this, with a kid or two involved as well. Of course, they would have to figure that out, but for now, this was good. The only person missing was Red.

Sebastian's heart raced, and his skin warmed at the knock on the door.

"Would you look at that? His marks nearly glow," Levi said with pride.

"Just like mine still does for you, Levi."

"Uh, Sebby." Mavis gaped.

"Okay, I forgot to tell you something."

Mavis nodded, her eyes wide. "I think so, but don't worry. Whatever the fuck this is, Cassie and I have your back. Shit, you're glowing, Sebby. Glowing." She stressed the last word

Sebastian was sorry for scaring the shit out of his friend, but he was more eager to get to the door.

CHAPTER FIFTEEN

Okay, so maybe Red had played a little dirty. Still, the idea to send his family in as relationship rescue was pretty fucking brilliant. He would typically hesitate to tell them anything about the person he was with, yet in desperation, he'd filled them in on every detail. No way he was losing Sebastian to his fears of Red's family discarding him because he was gay.

Nope. Ain't gonna happen.

When he'd gone home and paced back and forth trying to figure out what to do, then weeks later not getting anywhere, his mom called. She just knew. And Red never hid anything from her, so emptying coffers to share every detail with her hadn't been a burden. When he'd finished, she suggested breakfast with his mate and his family. Red had said yes, and trusting his family, had agreed to their request to have some time alone with him first.

Now, Red stood at the door and listened. Inside he heard laughter and the comfortable rumble of his father's voice. He smiled.

He knocked, and seconds later, Sebastian yanked open the door, his cheeks flushed. His eyes were even darker than the last time he'd seen him, his hair carelessly styled, and the baggy t-shirt he was wearing with a pair of grey sweats did something for Red's beast.

Red reached in and dragged him into the hall. Then he kissed him, hard and possessive, owning his mouth and savoring all the flavors of his mother's cooking combined with his mate's unique taste.

When he had his fill, he released Sebastian's mouth only to bring him closer, enjoying the hardness of his mate's dick against his mate's body. His mouth watered for a taste of that, too, but he could wait. He would have to.

"That was sneaky," Sebastian whispered.

"Yeah, well, all's fair." Red ran his lips along Sebastian's neck, nipping at the flesh he wanted to sink his teeth into again, renewing his claim. "My marks are glowing for me, Sebastian. You needed me."

Red could feel it all and loved every bit of it.

Sebastian's heart raced, his breathing harsh. Then, on a whine when Red's hand slipped beneath his sweatshirt, he managed to moan, "I don't know if I *needed* you."

"Sebastian, my marks on your flesh are like a lie detector. You can't lie to me, baby, and you can't lie to yourself, either. Your body's wanting me, mate. Your soul's crying out for me to take care of you right now."

Nothing compared to feeling what he needed from Sebastian, the way his heart echoed the beating of his mate's or the way his blood rushed through his veins from just being next to him, holding him.

Sebastian whimpered. "You sent your family."

"Had to." Red licked into Sebastian's mouth again, running his tongue across his teeth. "Didn't want you trying to deny me entry into your body and your soul because of fear. Best thing for it was to get them all over here."

Sebastian laughed and snuggled further into Red's embrace. "But—"

"No buts, baby. Once I told my mom what you were thinking, she just needed to know where you lived, and my father was on board. Didn't expect Jacobi to come, but nothing happened without Jacobi's input. He sniff you?"

"Oh, my goodness. Yes. Why?"

"It's a part of him, his ability to uncover truths, like a reader. Or like a hound dog. He's different. No explaining it, but we love him anyway."

"Hey! I'm not a hound dog," Jacobi huffed from around the corner. "Stop making out with your mate back there. We can all hear you and smell his need, too. Well, except for his bestie in here. But then she has her own questions."

"Sure do, Sebby. So fan those flames, and let's chat."

Sebastian dropped his head onto Red's chest, his words muffled. "This is my life."

"Our life, Sebastian. This is our life." Red held his mate tighter and kissed the top of his head.

"Haven't said yes to all of this, Red."

"I know. Just a matter of time." He smiled as they joined the others in the kitchen.

Sebastian wasn't surprised when Cassandra showed up. Mavis had messaged her as soon as she'd seen Sebastian glowing, she'd said. It was how they'd operated for years. No secrets.

"So, you're all griffins," Cassandra asked.

"Yes," Levi answered.

"Well, except for me, sweetheart. I'm human," Allice added.

"A witch," Jacobi corrected.

"Still human, sweetheart."

"Yes, ma'am. Just wanted her to know everything."

"Thank you, son."

Jacobi nodded and dipped his bread into the sweet glazed deliciousness on his plate, a soft smile on his face.

Although Sebastian only had eyes for Red, he had to admit Jacobi was a beautiful man with gilded hair and eyes that almost shimmered. Nevertheless, Sebastian felt warm, safe, and happy around Red's family, even if he was a little nervous about what his friends would think of everything.

"Okay, a witch. What type?" Cassandra asked.

"Green witch, darling," Alice answered and smiled.

"Okay, me, too. I'd read something in my tea leaves the other week. I wasn't sure which of us it meant. My husband is a dragon. Maybe the two of them could fly together some-time?"

"What the fuck, Cassie?" Sebastian looked at Mavis, who appeared just as shocked as him.

"In my defense, guys, I didn't know how you would take it. Isn't it nice to have so much in common? I mean, Mavis is human like us, and we have mates. Two out of three. If we work it right, we can get her a mate, then we're triplets, right?"

"Bitch," Mavis snapped.

"Okay, I heard that."

"I hope so, Cassandra Destiny Alarie. I meant for you to," Mavis chewed out.

"So, yeah. We can hash this out later. Right now, I'm more interested in why griffins are so far away from a clan. As far as I know, it's just the four of you."

While Sebastian tried to absorb Cassandra's mind-blowing news, his new family shared their story.

Later that night, Sebastian snuggled silently in the circle of Red's arms on the bed in front of the television. Everyone had gone home, leaving Sebastian's refrigerator filled with fresh produce and meat. Prepared meals with instructions sat on shelves — bottles of preserves stocked in his pantry. Promises of future visits were made, and he received a tight hug from each of them as they left, Levi squeezing him as he ordered him to drop by later to see his son's home.

Sebastian smiled. "I like this."

"What," Red asked.

"I like your family coming by. I like sitting here holding you while we watch whatever this is."

"It's part of the Marvel series."

"I don't remember this, but I do remember her. Why is everything in black and white, and how did she get babies so fast?"

"Just watch."

"I'd rather you put your cock in my ass."

Sebastian giggled when Red immediately turned the television off.

Red turned and crawled over Sebastian. "Oh, baby, that can be arranged."

Sebastian stretched out across the bed, his shorts shifting with a gap wide enough for Red to slip his hand inside. He caressed the warm velvety skin of his mate's shaft, and tugged on his soft pliable balls.

Red's beast ground against his mind, eager to claim and possess.

"You make me crazy, Red. I had to control myself so long, be someone different to keep my heart safe."

Red swallowed Sebastian's words, kissing him deeply and savoring the entirely Sebastian flavor.

Sebastian wrapped his arms behind Red's shoulders, pulling him on top. He bent his knees, splaying his lower body for Red.

Red was only too happy to oblige Sebastian by trailing his fingers over his mate's skin, touching him everywhere.

"I would only give bits of myself, the parts that wouldn't hurt. Be my loudest, fiercest, funniest, shiniest self. But inside, I hid the rest, the longing and the pain." He moaned. "Yes, Red, please there."

Red wasn't sorry for ripping Sebastian's heavy sweatshirt from his supple frame. With Sebastian's torso on display, Red's marks lit up like his personal Christmas tree with Sebastian as his gift.

He worked on removing Sebastian's shorts to get to his hard dick, precum already dampening his underwear. Red squeezed the length firmly in a grip tight.

"I need you, Red," Sebastian pleaded.

"I'm here, baby. I'm always going to be here. No matter what. Not gonna let you run me off."

"But you sent your family, Red."

Sebastian gasped when Red took a nipple in his mouth and bit down on the tender flesh, squeezing Sebastian's dick even tighter. He flicked the crown and smiled against his mate's skin when he whined.

"Anything, Sebastian. I would do anything to keep you, to keep this."

Red placed a finger on Sebastian's lips. "Get this wet for me, sweetie, sloppy wet. Gonna use you hard, Sebastian. Show you who owns you."

"Fuck," Sebastian took the digit into his mouth, sucking on Red's fingers, licking them thoroughly.

Red kissed his cheek. "Good job, baby. You done real good." A harsh tug, and Red tore Sebastian's underwear. The silky fabric didn't stand a chance against his need to be inside Sebastian.

Red shoved Sebastian's legs open wider and retook his mouth.

"Going to fuck you, baby."

Sebastian kissed Red this time. "Not going to stop you, Red. Can't wait to feel you inside."

"You could stop me if you wanted to. Just a word, a hand against my skin, and I would wait for you. I don't care how long. Just being next to you is enough."

Red needed Sebastian to understand that while he craved every inch of him, he would wait. Blue balls didn't matter. Dick hard enough to chip ice didn't matter. Sebastian was what mattered to him.

"No."

Red nodded, too eager to show his mate he could and would keep his word.

"No? Okay. We can watch a movie. I've wanted to check out that new Marvel series, or we can watch whatever you want. Don't much matter to me. Just as long as I'm with you." Red's cock had another opinion entirely, hard and leaking, and far too interested in settling between Sebastian's round cheeks.

Sebastian's eyes brightened with warmth before clutching Red to him tightly. "No, no waiting. No Marvel show unless you want to see it later. But oh, baby. That's the sweetest thing anyone's ever said to me. And being next to you means everything to me, too. But right now? Right now, all I want is you so deep inside my body that I can barely breathe with the fullness of you."

Sebastian's words had Red's beast humming inside, and he quaked with the need to have his mate beneath him. Rising over Sebastian's body, he let his gaze roam over his frame, taking in his flushed skin and beating pulse. He loved seeing his marks decorating Sebastian's throat and chest, and almost regretted when Sebastian wore a shirt, keeping them from his view.

He kissed Sebastian again, then stood to take off his clothes.

"You are so beautiful, Red. Did you know that? I love looking at you, and no matter what I told myself about letting you go, it was a lie. I don't think I'm strong enough to sacrifice what this could be. I'm selfish. Too selfish to do your words justice or make you prove something I already want all for myself."

Red smiled, taking the weight of his cock in his hand and fisting its length. "Be selfish with me, Sebastian. Want me for yourself. I like that. My beast loves that I'm who you need."

Sebastian smiled.

"Come here. Take my dick down your throat. Get me wet."

Sebastian nodded and quickly turned to crawl to Red.

Suddenly, Red's griffin pushed forward, presenting itself, ready to claim. "There you are, my sweet thing. My lovely creature." His mouth widened as his canines fell, his breathing was harsh now, words challenging to purse out. He crawled between Sebastian's legs, hungry to show his mate what he meant to him, what this moment meant to him.

Sebastian's head slammed back against the pillow when Red swallowed him from crown to root, the sharpness of his canines sliding over the fragile skin of Sebastian's beautiful dick.

"Oh, Red," Sebastian begged.

His mate's whimpers and pleas were magic to Red's ears, a call to his griffin. He happily sank his nose into the triangle of Sebastian's thighs, breathing in the glorious scent, enjoying the moans and writhing as Sebastian struggled against him. He stroked his tongue underneath Sebastian's length, playing with his lover's frenulum and savoring his mate's taste.

"Need you, Red. Inside. Fuck. Now. Please, Red."

Sebastian's cries were wrecked, his moans desperate, and Red's scalp ached from the grip Sebastian had on his hair. But none of that mattered.

He stuck his finger in with his mouth alongside Sebastian's cock, slurping at the digit while making certain he didn't leave the delicious muscle lacking. Once they were good and wet, he snaked his hand down below Sebastian's balls and worked his finger inside his lover's tight heat.

"Yes, Red. More. Please."

Red nodded and twisted his fingers inside, widening the space, getting Sebastian ready for him. Red wasn't small, and with his beast's need to claim his mate, he was certain he'd doubled in size. He refused to hurt Sebastian, so they would both have to be patient.

Sebastian rocked underneath him, pushing himself down on Red's fingers, more than one this time and deeper into Red's throat.

"You're going to make me come, Red."

Sebastian pushed against him, trying to free himself, but he was stronger. He sucked harder, reveling in Sebastian's spicy flavor. Sebastian spilled more precum, and Red feasted on his new favorite dessert.

Red released Sebastian's dick from between his lips with a pop. "It's okay, baby. I got you. Don't worry." He pulled his fingers from Sebastian's quivering hole, laving them with his tongue loving his lover's taste, then shoved them back in deeper, stretching his fingers wide.

Red wanted to do so many things with Sebastian, to him, but there would be time for all of it . . . later. What Red wanted now, hell, what he needed was to be balls deep in his mate's body. He needed to feel Sebastian's walls coated in his seed.

"Are you ready, sweetheart? Ready for that hole of yours to swallow my dick, squeeze it with your muscles?"

Red stood, smiling from Sebastian's enraptured expression while his eyes traced over Red's pecs, his arms, and down to his waist. He did a little shimmy, keeping his one-eyed monster targeted on Sebastian.

"Let me see how gorgeous that hole of yours is, baby. Spread your legs and open up."

Sebastian wasn't shy in the least, quickly honoring Red's wish. "Whatever gets you moving faster." He pointed his toes as he stretched his legs wide.

Red almost drooled when he saw the red pucker displayed

just for him, open and ready after the prep he had done. Leaning over to grab his pants, he retrieved a lube packet, opening it quickly.

"Not too much, Red. I like the burn, and from your expert job earlier, I'm ready."

"Are you sure, Sebastian? I don't want to hurt you."

"Red, I like a little pain. Come on. Get that dick over here, *querido*."

Red's face warmed. "I'm your darling, Sebastian?"

"Yeah, Red. You are. Now come on."

Red nodded, all hesitation gone now. After swiping some slick on the round mushroom head of his dick, he tossed the packet and grabbed Sebastian's legs. He settled between those muscular thighs and pushed forward until his head was in, then sank deep and hard, Sebastian's ass swallowing his entire length.

"Shit," Sebastian growled. "You are so fucking big, Red. I don't remember you filling me up as much as this. I can hardly breathe with so much dick inside me."

"I know, Sebastian. I know. Deep breath, and take all of me, okay. Deep breath. There you go. That's it. Oh, yeah. I'm totally in now. All in, sweetheart."

Sebastian's head fell back when Red paused and praised him. He knew he was longer and wider than before, but he couldn't help himself. His griffin responded to the claiming and meant to lock Sebastian to him. When Sebastian let out a long sigh of air and trembled, it was like the trigger his griffin needed. Claws exploded from Red's fingertips, and he spun Sebastian on the end of his dick to his hand and knees. He coiled himself around his mate with grunts and growls more animal than man.

"Shit, Red." Sebastian shook.

Red impaled him relentlessly, his wings itching for release, their coupling overwhelming him. He moaned with a growl.

The sound must have spoken to Sebastian. "Whatever you need, Red. Do it. Take me."

Something crashed to the floor when Red's wings opened, bathing the room in darkness. He ignored it, unable to stop. Pressing himself closer to his mate, he covered them, cocooning them both. He used a knee to spread Sebastian's legs further apart, and his beast did its best to make them one living, throbbing organism.

When Sebastian began to shake with his orgasm, his cries and moans a reflection of his pleasure, Red struck, sinking his canines into Sebastian's nape. When Sebastian fell back, Red caught him and held him, drinking, and fucking until he too released, and they both drifted into the darkness.

CHAPTER SIXTEEN

"You want to take me flying?" Sebastian asked.

They'd settled on Thai for dinner, picking it up after going to a movie. Boxes were put away after savoring pineapple chicken curry, steamed pork dumplings, and seafood noodle soup. The air was still thick with lovely spices, both from the food they'd enjoyed along with the heady aroma of their lovemaking. And now, as they so often found themselves lately, they were lying in Red's bed with sheets twisted around their legs.

Sebastian wouldn't admit to Red that it was his favorite place to be, even though he was sure Red knew it. He spent more time at Red's place than his own recently. And how many times had Red hinted that he should cancel his lease? But it was his, and he liked the idea of having something of his own, a fallback plan.

I mean, really? Shouldn't a person always have a fallback plan?

"Yes, baby. I want to take you flying. You've seen me often enough."

Red was gorgeous when he took to the sky, his head in the clouds and wings buffeting the air. He was majestic, a gift, and Sebastian loved watching him soar.

"I have," but that didn't mean Sebastian wanted to fly with him.

Red had taken advantage of the forest behind Sebastian's place to introduce his griffin. The beast was lovely, standing as tall as an elephant, dragon-like wings spreading wide. And the view of his golden lion's body did things to Sebastian that shouldn't be acceptable. He nearly came when Red's golden gaze peered deep into his soul. How many times had he crouched for Sebastian, inviting him to ride?

But while Sebastian might be fine with flight in a lovely large airplane, he was not interested in taking to the clouds without being surrounded by metal, mate or not.

"You should want to fly with me. I'm your mate. You should trust me to take care of you." Red pouted adorably.

Sebastian climbed onto Red's lap, leaning down to kiss him under his chin and lick at his throat. He smiled when Red slid a claw down his spine, grasping his naked hip.

"Baby, in the weeks we've been together I've gone mudding with you in your truck, helped you bring a new foal into the world with your family. Truly disgusting but so beautiful. I mean, wow. We've gone camping, and I promise you, that is not something I would ever have done before. While I appreciate the great outdoors, I don't necessarily want to be a part of it. All these things took time, okay? Well, maybe not the filly, because my little girl was ready to be born but unsure of which way to go. I sort of compare riding you in the open sky—with the possibility of slipping off and falling to my death—with climbing on the back of a motorcycle without protection. I like doors, seats, and windows."

When Sebastian would have scooched back to take Red into his mouth, his mate pulled him forward instead, kissing him.

"No, I know what you're doing."

Okay, so maybe he was trying to distract him, but he would have absolutely followed through.

"I don't know what you're talking about."

Sebastian loved Red's laugh. It was powerful and free. So whenever Red laughed, he did, too.

How long had he needed this and simply hadn't known what was missing? To have someone check on him, wait for him at the airport, take him home, prepare a bath for him, massage his tired body, and put him to bed after making sure he came hard enough to nearly blind himself? He wasn't allowed to forget to eat or neglect what he needed because Red was always there.

And while he loved his girls, spoke to them almost daily, having someone there just for him made his heart sing.

But he wasn't getting on Red's back to go flying, no matter what he said.

"You know, baby. One day."

Sebastian giggled when Red reached for him. "One day, maybe, but for now, I'd rather taste you."

"Sebastian, oh baby. Fuck."

One could not always predict what the future could hold or determine what even the next few hours could bring. All Sebastian cared about at the moment was being wrapped up in the arms of the man he loved, safe, and replete. He was happy.

Sure, they were both covered in cum, legs twined together and sticky. Showers were in order, but they were both too satiated to care. While the fastidious nurse in him should feel utterly disgusted by the state of him and his lover, he reveled in the joy of wearing his mate's scent, and the way his marks glowed.

Unbelievably, he'd become accustomed to the marks and enjoyed the thrum that coursed through him when he thought of Red. He'd gotten better at dressing in a way that drew less attention to them. Hell, if necessary, he'd always say he'd gotten a new tattoo. It wasn't as if people would think otherwise.

When holes suddenly appeared in the walls, along with crashing and wooden splinters decorating the room like confetti, thought of his marks were pushed out of his mind.

"Fuck," Red growled, obviously more alert than Sebastian.

Shrugging off sleep didn't prove that difficult when the wooden column next to his head exploded. Suddenly Red grabbed him and pulled him off the bed, covering him with his own body.

"Red, what the hell is going on? What is this?"

"I don't know, but I have an idea. But first, let's get the hell out of here, okay?"

How the hell were they going to get out of it? Gunfire was obliterating Red's home, and Sebastian heard thuds of foot-steps in the other room. He tried to remember how many places there were to hide at Red's. Two bedrooms—one they were currently hiding in—a kitchen, a study, a mudroom. There was a connecting bathroom where he and Red had spent a lot of time. *Ah-ha, there's a window in there.*

Was that window large enough for them to get out?

Shit, could he even get to his gun? This wasn't a Bond movie, and he wasn't a superhero from a Marvel movie.

Sebastian glanced toward the beautiful bay window deco-rating Red's bedroom. If they could get to it, that might be the way out of this nightmare. He cringed at the thought of de-stroying the glass that Red had flown in special from Italy, each piece cut precisely to fit the arch.

The place was falling around them, and Sebastian looked around in a haze. Red's home didn't have much, some furni-ture, pots, and pans though Red didn't cook, and clothing. His man loved clothes, mostly plaid and denim, although he owned some worn shorts, purposefully ripped in just the right places.

He had been gradually nesting in a way, making Red's lit-tle dark cement dungeon more of a home. The new bureau splintering before his eyes held some of his clothing and a few items he'd planned as a surprise for Red. The two of them were becoming a little more adventurous in the bedroom, and the treasure trove of supplies he was preparing would have been fun to play with.

The mirror that shattered on the wall was a recent addition. Sebastian remembered selecting it himself that day on Frankfurt Avenue, a street littered with store after store of unusual finds. Walking into Manor Happenings that day had been a treat, and when he'd eyed the over six-foot slat of glass bordered by bronze, he had to have it.

Red loved to stand in front of the mirror with Sebastian on his knees, his throat filled with Red's length. It was one of Sebastian's favorite moments.

Sebastian recalled fucking Red, watching their reflection. Red's freckled skin blushing all over, his red hair sweaty and spiked, his breaths matching Sebastian's. Red asked for Sebastian to love him, and while being a top hadn't been his position of choice, he would do anything to please his lover. Well, anything except fly. That was non-negotiable.

"Sebastian, baby. Snap out of it. Are you okay?"

Right, memory lane is not where I need to be right now. Much more important to focus on the people trying to kill us.

Especially when they were about to be fighting for their lives.

"Sebastian!"

"I'm okay, Red. I'm okay. What are we going to do?"

"Okay, first we have to get out of the house and away. There are too many of them for us to fight."

"I have my gun."

"Baby, I have several, and none of those are going to help us right now. Best thing for us to do is retreat."

There was an eerie pause to the gunfire, but the footsteps were still moving through the home, searching.

"The window," Red whispered.

It was dark, but Sebastian could see his lover. And he knew the moment Red had decided just what needed to be done.

"No," Sebastian said.

"Baby. No choice right now. I knew I'd get you to ride me

one day. Now, let's break that fucking window and get the hell out of here before they get in."

Breaking a window was not as easy as it looked. Tempered, thick, and gorgeous, it was a puzzle of several dimensions. When a bullet suddenly shattered the glass, it was just enough for the two of them to charge through.

Sebastian fell and spun, but Red didn't hesitate, instantly shifting into the fantastic creature he was, his wings battering the wind as he flew beneath Sebastian amid flying bullets.

Sebastian was terrified, but he trusted his mate and held on tight to his fur, fingers buried into the muscle. "Where are we going to go?"

Home was the word that traveled to his mind. Warmth followed it, embracing Sebastian's chilled body.

Uncertain about their path but glad to be on their way to safety, he settled in for the ride.

CHAPTER SEVENTEEN

"Do you see smoke, Red?" Sebastian asked. Red's fears echoed in his mate's voice, and he tensed at the sight before him.

Chaos and terror.

They had escaped one nightmare only to find themselves in another.

"Faster, Red! We need to help!" In a t-shirt and not much else, Sebastian leaped from Red's back.

Red refused to lose his mate in his effort to help. Instead, he shifted quickly, capturing Sebastian in the air and setting him down gently before they both took off running.

"Look for my parents while I try to save the barn and free the animals," Red shouted. The smoke was thick and heavy, worse than anything he'd seen before.

Flames licked the grounds at their feet, and the homestead Red had grown up on was in shambles. Grabbing Sebastian to him for a wrenching kiss, he turned toward the barn. He could hear the fearful cries of the animals. There were four horses, plus the recently born filly Sebastian had adopted as his spoiled baby and named her Lilac. It would kill his lover to lose the filly, so Red needed to get there first.

He knew his father would take care of his mother no matter what happened. To him, it would mean more for Sebastian's skills to be there to help them.

He arrived at the barn, but the metal was hot enough to sear human fingers. Switching to claws and using his griffin strength, he tore the door from the hinges and stormed into the building. First he opened the stall to his parents' horses, Calliope, and Rising Star. Their eyes were wide as they looked around, struggling to find their way in the darkness. He cooed to them and pushed them gently toward the open door. They were frantic, but they knew him and trusted his voice. Then more concerned about the new mother and her foal, he hurried Calliope and Rising Star along with a slap on their rumps, and they took off, the thunder of their hooves slapping the ground.

Red vaguely heard other voices, some he recognized from nearby farms. He trusted the horses to have found aid. If not, he'd round them up later. He turned toward the inner recess of the stable.

"Butterscotch," he called to his horse, who was striking the door. His baby was protective of his mate, Jacobi's horse, Leaps-a-lot. They'd been together for years, and he'd laughed at his horse's antics when courting the Appaloosa. He'd gotten her, though, and had a beautiful foal for his trouble.

"I'm here, big guy. I've got you." Butterscotch slammed himself against the stall wildly. "Shh, big daddy. Them first, I understand. I'll get them out, and then you, okay?" A beam crashed, and Red's heart raced with urgency. They were surrounded by wood and straw. It was a matchbox ready to go up in flames, and it didn't help that the smoke was coming in thick and heavy.

As if he understood every word, the horse settled down but still paced the length of the stall he shared alongside Leaps-a-lot, who was frighteningly quiet. Jacobi's horse was an energetic Appaloosa. She was also a beautiful mother who doted on her foal. Sebastian had helped save mother and baby when she was giving birth, but he was a nurse, not a veterinarian. However, his lover was resourceful, so he'd called for help and was able to bring a new life into the world, one that would crush his mate to lose.

Red opened the stall, but mother and foal were lying still. "Shit." He fell to his knees and shook them both while Butterscotch neighed loudly with fear.

"It's going to be okay. Just need to get you out of here. Get you some fresh air, sweetie."

"Red!" Jacobi shouted.

Red let out a sigh, thankful, because if anyone could help get a mother and her young out of a burning building, his built like a double-sided fridge little brother could.

"In here, at the back. Where's Sebastian?"

In moments, Jacobi knelt beside him, hand running over the horses carefully.

"He's fine, brother. Balls and sausage exposed, but I don't think he realizes it, too intent on helping mother care for those caught in this blaze. Grabbed him a pair of shorts. What can I do to help?"

Sebastian, unwittingly half-naked but still trying to save lives, distracted him for half a second before Lilac's soft whimpering whipped him back to the task at hand.

"All right then, we have to get them all out. Butterscotch is fine, just upset about his girls. Mother and foal are particularly quiet, which is worrisome. Thinking we need to get them out of here and into some fresh air."

The smoke was thickening and beginning to wreak havoc with his throat.

"That cough of yours ain't helping, Red. Let's get it together and get everyone out of here." Jacobi stood.

Suddenly it struck Red how looking at Jacobi was like looking at royalty. Jacobi was his younger brother, but how often had he and his family bent themselves to his will? How many of their people had fallen under his spell, bringing whole families to live next to them?

Red's vision became crystal clear as he watched the way Jacobi cradled Lilac's body to his chest and walked out the doorway. *How fucking incredible is that?*

Butterscotch suddenly tore out the other side of the barn. Red followed, hearing cheers outside as many sought to help Jacobi. Instead, his brother shouted for water for Red and a blanket to wrap the filly in.

Jacobi always had a penchant for taking care of his people, and the way he protected all the lives on their land was part of his nature. Was that it? Was it remembering how Jacobi had visited each of the families now standing around them and knowing that each of these people shared whatever goods and serviced they could with Red's family because of Jacobi? Was it the way they looked at Jacobi with hope and love? Or was Red seeing Jacobi in a new light because he'd fallen in love with Sebastian, their bond realized?

No, it was more than that. Now, what the hell to do with what he knew to be true?

And what did they do with the people climbing out of cars surrounding them now, people with guns flanking a man who Red's father had been trying to keep them safe from for years?

"So many years and nothing, Levi Redmond Enyalius. We honored your request for separation, and then we find you have established a sanctuary. One where others of our kind have chosen to follow you as if you are king, the Ilios of our people." The Ilios paced slowly.

Laith Baher was slender, and while he appeared young, Red knew the man was much older. He was also beautiful, an almost angelic appearance with curly, golden hair that fell to his shoulders. He and those he arrived with wore similar suits, expensive and well-cut. The luxurious cars they drove and the posh clothing were strong indicators of the wealth the Ilios had accumulated.

Sebastian looked down from the ruin of Red's family home

to where a man shouted across the grass at the people gathered there, his lover and mate among them.

If he weren't so damned tired, this whole moment would have been funny. Red's family thought they were alone, but this family who seemed to have lost everything was anything but. Here they were surrounded by their little kingdom. All around them were people Sebastian had met and spoken to, who asked about them, who sent gifts and fresh bread. Sebastian had stopped by their homes, had given advice, and offered medical help. They weren't just neighbors. They were a village.

At least fifty people stood by with food and water, towels and clothing, and love. Sebastian hadn't wanted to be separated from Red, but his lover had trusted him to take care of his family, find them and do what he did best if they needed medical care. And he had done his best. All on his end were well. Red's mother, with her magic, was busy saving those caught in the fiery damage. Together, they'd healed and secured wounds, wiped tears, and returned little ones to nervous arms. No one lost. Not one. And Sebastian had been a part of that.

He was a part of a family, and he had Red to thank for that.

Seeing Red and knowing he was safe filled him with joy. His mate. Sebastian's marks called to him, but then he'd noticed a man more gorgeous than any supermodel standing there with a group of others as they exited large, high-end SUVs, forming a semi-circle around the family and the people with them.

"The Ilios has arrived here on our land." Alice was suddenly standing beside him. "I'm fairly certain he's the reason why Red's house was destroyed along with our farm. He's been watching us and knew when Red found his mate."

"Me?" Sebastian said. "All this loss is because of me?"

Alice brought him close, her hand on his wrist.

"No, Sebastian. No. There were signs of their encroachment long before you arrived. This is because of Ilios Laith Baher's desire to change his role from one of honor to one of suffering and manipulation. This Ilios doesn't care about protecting others. He doesn't care about community and family. He is a griffin in body only, an Ilios in title alone. And he is afraid."

But the man who appeared larger than life, who stood with an entourage of beautiful men and women, didn't seem afraid. He came off as calm and collected. Sebastian had expected evil personified, someone from a horror movie. Instead, the Ilios shared a friendly smile calling out to Red's father as if they were old friends.

Sebastian didn't trust those types of smiles.

Catty bitch smiles.

"I am here." Levi strode forward fearlessly. Tired, dirty, and covered in soot but not broken, he walked out to stand across from the Ilios. His red hair was streaked with gray and resembled more a lion's mane, his clothing covered in ash a stark contrast. But he was not any less for it. He raised his hand, switching to claw and back, then bowed his head. "We've done nothing but take care of our family and our home. Staying away from you and yours as agreed. We did not ask for our people to find us. We kept our distance."

"Yes, your distance but not your promise, for your young has found his mate, and I do not have him returned to us, the gift that should be at the arm of every griffin leader. And look around you. My people stand beside you, following a leader who should be at my home, securing our grounds and helping us to grow. But instead, you have pulled them to your side."

"I have asked for none of these people to stand with us."

"And yet here they are," a woman said, moving forward. "I told the Ilios such a thing could happen. People lured by the promise of power would follow the light."

"Who is she," Sebastian asked, his heart in his throat. The whole day had been rough enough with first Red's house then his family home. And now, here they were in some type of standoff.

"She is the Atkina, ray of the sun," Alice said. "I do not doubt that she was the one who ordered Red's home attacked and our farm burned to the ground, she and the Stemma, the men and women who act as the Ilios's corona."

"Ilios?"

"Sun. Clan leader. That man down there is supposed to be the keeper of knowledge and wisdom, a treasure of the world. But instead, he's used the power at his hand to subjugate and terrorize others. He wants my son, your mate, so he can keep his power, not for growth but as a part of his horde."

The Atkina stepped forward. "I am the Atkina, ray to the sun, who should be the voice of our people, the keeper of wisdom and knowledge, the wealth of our people. He protects and guards you, enables you to progress, to be a part of a family that will light the world. But instead of following him, paying tribute, you have aligned yourselves with those who have deserted their Ilios." She was a tall woman, holding her head high, a long blonde braid hanging over her back. She wore a tailored suit with a sharp pair of boots that Sebastian would die to own.

A voice cried out from the people on his mate's side. "Since when have the Ilios and his Stemma had to use violence against his people? We gave tribute to provide for those who could not care for themselves, our orphans, and the broken. But you took the money we work so hard for and did not support us. Instead, you used us."

"You are not to question the Ilios," one of the Stemma shouted back before pulling an automatic rifle and aiming it at the speaker.

Those standing near the speaker moved forward, a wall of

solidarity. "We are no longer afraid of you and your weapons. We have a new light. A new sun whose light will shine brighter than your own."

"Do you? Show us. Can you tell us who the Ilios is to be, Levi?" the Ilios asked kindly.

"No, Ilios. My son has his mate, and that gift has passed from me."

"Then it would appear that you are no of no use to us," the Ilios said. "Let's see what the people can do without their hero."

The Ilios's shift to a griffin was in the blink of an eye, but Jacobi shifted faster and stood before Levi. His claws dug deep within Ilios's throat, tearing down and away. Finally, the Ilios fell to the ground, and his Stemma swooped in prepared to fight, the Atkina leading them.

When chaos erupted, Red's voice rose above all others.

CHAPTER EIGHTEEN

"Listen to me! I am Docent, mated, and seer of the line. My mate bears my marks!"

Red's birthright had arrived, and he had failed to notice, but there had been signs all along. If only he'd paid attention, they might have been able to save their land, not forced to rebuild, but none of that mattered anymore.

The former Atkina called to him, enraged over the attack of the Ilios, seething for bloodshed. "You lie. Show us the marks. Bring your mate to us, Docent, and show us that you are not simply trying to save the life of your nestmates. See if these so-called marks will give us the light. If they cannot, we will take the lives of everyone here from adult to child."

She stretched her arm, and the Stemma fanned around the fallen Ilios prepared for battle. The Ilios's breaths were shallow, but he would live. Red was more concerned about making sure his family did, too.

"Sebastian!" Red called.

His mate did not hesitate, running full tilt down the hill from where his mother and the younger children remained safe.

Red opened his arms to welcome Sebastian and held him tightly, breathing him in. "My love. My mate. I need you."

Sebastian kissed him, dirty fingers wiping at his tears. "Whatever you need, I promise I'll give. I'm all in."

"You are the light, the one who my power shines through. Your marks will find the next Ilios, and while I know with all my heart, who it is, none will believe without seeing. I need you, Sebastian. Be my vessel,"

Sebastian pulled back and took a breath. "I trust you, Red. I'm not sure what being your vessel means, but if it saves you and the family I love as my own, I will be whatever you need me to be."

The Atkina screamed. "Fuck all of this talking and display the marks. Show us the light or die!"

Metal flew in the air, and a gasp was heard before a body fell to the ground.

Several in the crowd screamed. "No!"

"Now, Docent, or more lives will be lost!"

Red took a deep breath and stepped back from Sebastian. "Sebastian, please take off your clothes and bare my marks to our people."

Sebastian, bless him, stripped immediately, fully naked for all to see. He trembled in cold the air, but he was glorious and brave without knowing what Red would need of him. He obviously loved Red enough to be a sacrifice for him and his family.

It was a gift Red would treasure for the rest of his life.

"Our Ilios is Jacobi Redmond Enyalius, and the light of my mate, Sebastian Del Marco, who bears my mark, will reveal the sun for all."

To Sebastian, he whispered, "Breathe through this, baby. You are glorious. Thank you."

Red shifted into his beast and sank his claws into his mate's sides, holding him tightly. Sebastian's screams reached inside Red, and the need to taste and drink burned. He turned his beak to the side so he could open fully to consume his mate's essence and rejoice in the light. His beacon rose from their joining and positioned above his brother's head, the new Ilios, the new keeper of the sun.

His mate was enflamed, and Red wanted to be inside him,

wanted to take him before everyone and show them his ownership. Claim. Fuck. Drink. They were a conduit, and together they would burn.

"Your light burns, Docent. We see and honor the new Ilios," a voice said from among the Stemma.

Red continued to drink as all around them shifted to griffins kneeling, eagle heads bowed, giving honor to the new Ilios, the new light.

"Shit." Jacobi nodded, looking around in wonder, then turned to Red. "Release your mate, my brother. We are safe, and you are freed of your task. Carry your prize away and return to us anew."

Red lifted quickly into the air with his wings spread, his prey between his claws.

They wove in the air, Sebastian's blood slippery, but Red would never let him fall. Sebastian belonged to him.

Sebastian was on fire, his entire body needing relief. He whimpered and moaned as licks of energy stampeded over his skin.

"Shh, baby. I'm here."

That was what he needed, who he needed. His mate. He reached for the voice, opening himself to his lover's touch, welcoming him inside and crying out in joy when they were one.

"You were so good today, Sebastian. So good. You glowed."

Sebastian warmed at his lover's praise, sighing from delicious kisses, loving the nibbles along his neck.

"You love me."

Sebastian laughed softly, gasping when Red started fucking him hard and long, praising him as he took and gave. "Yes, baby. I do. I love you."

"Yes. I love you, too. Seeing you present my marks, being my vessel. I couldn't wait to get inside you. Open your legs wider," Red growled. "Honey, I'm sorry. This won't be long. I can't. I need to come inside you, fill you so good, my seed leaking out of your hole. Claim you. They all saw you, saw what is mine, and if I don't fill you right the fuck now, I'm going to lose my mind."

Red's kisses grew more demanding, rougher. Sebastian knew the moment Red was ready to bite.

"Whatever you need, Red. Always."

Blades slid into his skin, the fire lancing him where Red took greedy gulps. He rocked into Red's movements, his arms around Red's shoulders and pressing his neck deeper, submitting to his lover.

Too much and too soon, his cum erupted from his dick and over his belly, Red quickly following behind.

Together they fell asleep, holding each other tightly.

When Sebastian awoke, it was to Red licking the inside of his thigh.

Sebastian sighed, stretching languorously. "What are you doing?"

"Ain't it obvious? I'm watching my come slide out of your hole and tasting your ass."

Sebastian shivered.

"Love when you do that, baby. Never knew the mouthy thing I met in a gun class would make me feel the way you do."

"And how's that?" Sebastian asked.

"Like I would give my soul for you. You were brave today, Sebastian. I told you I needed you, and you were there." Red gazed at him with pride.

Sebastian couldn't look away. "I always will be."

"I believe you. Thank you for being my vessel. You were

my light. My soul was yours. It still is."

"I felt it. Your love. I still do."

Everything in Red lay bare before Sebastian. They had no secrets between them. It was a new sensation for Sebastian, this transparency. But he wasn't afraid. He wanted it, craved it. His mate, his family, and his future.

Two nights ago, he and his girls had gone for tacos because why not? They'd gotten over their secrets and made playdates for their guys, which Sebastian was going to tell Red about when he was ready.

More importantly, he was happy to tell Mavis and Cassandra he was ready for the next steps with his mate. Prepared to live with Red and make some babies. Okay, they didn't have the parts, but surrogates and adoption existed for a reason.

"Sebby, honey. I'd be happy to have your little ones for you. Whatever you needed. You know that, right?" Fuck, Sebastian had cried, big snot-filled-wailers, welcoming the hugs of the sisters of his heart.

"I'd help you adopt, babe. My doors are locked, sealed, and barred, but I know people who know people. You just give us the go-ahead," Cassandra said as she wiped at his tears.

Family. He had a family. He wasn't alone anymore. Maybe his father would come around, and perhaps he could see his mother and his blood relatives without so much pain and regret. Because he was whole. He was whole.

He had a future and people who loved him. Of course, they weren't perfect, and some weren't even human. But they were his.

EPILOGUE

"When were you going to tell me, Red," Jacobi ground out as he stalked the floor.

"I wasn't sure myself, Jacobi. I'd only just put things together before everything went down," Red answered.

Jacobi's hair was a mess, his fingers having worn wild paths through it as he paced. They were all sitting in Sebastian's living room. Sebastian was the perfect host, filling drinking glasses as Red's mother passed around plates of food.

Levi stood near the window, staring at his sons.

"I'm a farmer. I was born to take care of our land," Jacobi insisted.

Levi sighed. "And you will, son. Just not the way any of us suspected. An Ilios in the Docent bloodline. I would never have believed it. But then, think about it. In the last two years, we've had more of our people move next to us, and while I've done my best to keep us separate, I know you've been providing for them. So tell me I'm lying, son."

Jacobi sighed and dropped to take Levi's seat. "They needed us, dad. And I couldn't *not* help them. They had nothing."

"And as the Ilios, our sun, you were there to give aid. It's what an Ilios does. Perhaps if the last Ilios had remembered his duty to his people, to his role, then he would still be alive."

Instead, the Ilios was dead, his existence snuffed out by his Stemma. Outside now, standing like sentries, the Stemma stood waiting for Jacobi's directive.

"I don't want this."

"Unfortunately, son, you don't have a say in this. You were chosen, and I think the choice was a good one. Throws a wrench in things with both the Ilios and the Docent coming from the same line, but I have to believe there's a reason for everything. Fortunately, Red got his head out of his ass in time enough for it to play out, and we're still here to see it."

"Levi!" Red's mother shouted.

"Sorry, Alice, but the boy was sticking his wick in every candle he could. Got a man now, his mate. Now, if he could get us some grandchildren . . . Hear that, Sebastian."

Red looked at Sebastian, whose face was red, but he could feel something along the thread that tied them. They had some talking to do.

"As for you, Ilios Jacobi Redmond Enyalius, it looks like you need to be finding your way in your new role. You'll need your own Atkina, since the last one died along with the Ilios. Rays require their sun to live. It's the way of it. Any thoughts?"

There wasn't an ounce of regret in his father's words. It was the way of things. No ray could live without the sun. It was their duty to be the right hand, and Jacobi would need someone ready to make the sacrifices necessary for a ray.

Red was more interested in the way Sebastian was avoiding his gaze. That talk needed to be had now, not later.

"Ilios, whatever you need, we are there to provide. And when you think about it, you've been telling us what to do since you were knee-hi to a grasshopper. You keep doing that. We'll all be fine," Red said.

Jacobi laughed and shook his head. "First thing we need to do is fix the farm and determine what it will take to get things repaired. Our livestock is housed elsewhere for now, but they're safe. Horses are fine. Land can be reseeded and nourished, and mom can use her magic to heal it. So this Ilios thing can wait until that, at least. And since there's no place else for us to sleep, Docent, looks like your mate's place is the perfect spot for all of us. So don't keep us up too late, okay."

Red smiled warmly. "Whatever you need. You have my word."

"You're the architect, and you have the resources. So I'll hold you to it."

"I've got you, Jacobi."

Jacobi sighed and stood, nodding. "Thank you. I'm grateful."

"Okay, then," his mother said, taking over. "The rooms have been determined. Let's all get some shut-eye and leave Sebastian and Red to it." She winked at Red with her knowing.

What is she up to?

Later, with Sebastian in his arms, the heat of their lovemaking still upon them, he listened as his mate explained his desire for a family. Unsure of how Red's father and mother might respond, Sebastian had asked Red's mother privately. His mate had been afraid of rejection, again, but Red's mother had shared happy tears, easing his fears.

When Sebastian finished, Red kissed him. "We don't need children for us to be a family, Sebastian. But wait, love," Red said when Sebastian moved away. "No. No, let me finish. We don't need children, my love, but to have them with you, to have babes with your gorgeous brown eyes, little flirty Sebastian doppelgangers would warm my heart. You are my heart, Sebastian Del Marco, future Sebastian Redmond Enyalius."

Sebastian wrapped his arms around Red's neck, and Red welcomed his touch, his love. He looked forward to the future they would share together.

ABOUT THE AUTHOR

Deja Black had fantasies of men loving men who felt strongly, loved hard, and needed a hero. Then one great day she came across a book and discovered the world of m/m writing, encountered others who shared her obsession as much as she did, and found a world where she could not only be accepted for the lives and loves she envisioned, but she could create them too. So why not? Why not take the stories she would write and throw away as a teenager, grow them, dream them, and make them a reality where she could let them live their story and make them real for someone else? And she did. Now, with the support of her hubby and some intense time management, she is learning to balance her family of two energetic children at home, along with the many students she counsels every day, as well as her passion for writing what she loves to read. Oh, and did you know she has two beautiful frogs now? Life is full of surprises.

Deja is always interested in connecting to new people who also share her love, so please feel free to contact her at:

Facebook: www.facebook.com/deja.black.69

Blog: https://dejablack77.blogspot.com/

Twitter: @DejaBlack69